Praise for Terry Cronin's
STUDENTS OF THE UNUSUAL

"Cronin has created a comic series which is **rich in atmosphere** and experiments freely with the line between horror and reality." -Prick Magazine

"Where others tend to shirk plot development duties and focus strictly on puns and twist conclusions (the latter being the requisite staple of the short story genre), Cronin makes great effort to **front-load surprise endings with bizarre cultural mythology**" -Rue Morgue Magazine

"Students of the Unusual is clearly **at the head of the class**, and at this pace will graduate with many honors!" -The Comic Fanatic

"Rarely have I read an anthology like *Students Of The Unusual* that is weird and funny and subtle and suspenseful and **makes me genuinely anticipate the next issue**... This is **storytelling in its purest form**" -Geeks of Doom

"A grasp of **mixing the scary with absurd humor** that Cronin has really refined quite well." - Comic's Waiting Room

"**Old-fashioned and clever**, and the story is witty." -Comic Buyer's Guide

Also by Terry Cronin

Recalcitrant Jones & the Dead Beats
Students of the Unusual

the SKINVESTIGATOR
TRAMP STAMP

TERRY CRONIN

Published by 3 Boys Productions
Copyright © 2010 by Terry Cronin

First Edition, Preview © July 2010 by Terry Cronin
Cover art by Luis Diaz. Photography by Steven Shea.
Logo and design by Gary Scott Beatty.

This is a work of fiction. Names, characters, places, and
incidents either are the product of the author's imagination or
are used fictitiously. Any resemblance to actual persons,
living or dead, events, or locales is entirely coincidental.

This book contains an excerpt from the forthcoming book
The Skinvestigator: Rash Guard by Terry Cronin. This
excerpt has been set for this edition only and may not reflect
the final content of the forthcoming edition.

ISBN: 978-0-9749266-8-1
www.3boysproductions.com
www.studentsoftheunusual.com

Printed in the United States of America

10 9 8 7 6 5 4 3 2

The Skinvestigator

Tramp Stamp

————————

TERRY CRONIN

Acknowledgements

I would like to thank a whole bunch of people for their support and encouragement. Special thanks to Ava, Mom, Dad, Terry III, Joe, Daniel, Gary Scott Beatty, Allison Bell, Scott Bell, Mike Broder, Aila Danielson, Luis Diaz, Kim Givens, Jeff Hall, Linda Hufnagel, Nina Keck, Katharine Leis, Bob Lizek, Pat Martin, Steven Shea, and Ed Yob. Thanks to editor Michael Garrett and to everyone who recognizes a little of themselves in my stories. The loss of my sister's beloved dog "Dude" provided inspiration for this story.

For Ava
the light of my life

1
"Soak Up the Sun" -Sheryl Crow

Miami Beach, nestled on the southeastern tip of Florida, has been "the" current destination for the young and old, rich and famous, and celebrity and paparazzi alike for a long time. People may come for the entertainment, food, and culture, but far and away Miami Beach was now the ideal location for sun, surf, and sand.

Lourdes Rivera loved being at the beach. She considered herself a "people watcher" and, besides soaking up the rays, she spent all her time happily wondering about where all the tourists came from. She wasn't enjoying herself today.

Normally she didn't mind men checking out her booty, but this guy was creepy. He kept staring at her and taking pictures. Lourdes Rivera had had enough, so she walked quickly across the sand to the lifeguard stand and looked up at the well-tanned and muscular professional. Miami Beach was well-known for fielding an athletic corps of lifeguards.

"Hey mister, can you help me?"

"That's what I'm here for, *señorita*."

"There's a strange man following me."

The lifeguard climbed down from his tower and stepped into the sand next to her.

"Can't say that I blame him, but point him out to me."

Lourdes turned her head to where the man was before and found that he had vanished.

"He's gone," she said.

The lifeguard smiled and noticed the small horse tattooed at the base of her spine. She felt his obvious admiration of her "tramp stamp" as he lifted his gaze and looked confidently into her eyes.

"Looks like he couldn't stand the competition," he said with a wink.

Lourdes felt the sun on her shoulders and smiled.

2
"Sunnyside of the Street" - The Pogues

"Sometimes you can feel these things more than you can see them. The pre-cancers will feel like a grit of sand or a little horn. If you let yourself get too horny, people will confuse you with Tiger Woods."

This always resulted in a jaw-dropping silent response and then a deep delayed laugh from every patient I used it on. Stock in trade icebreaker to put the patient at ease when they were seeing their dermatologist for a skin cancer check. I used to always end the joke with "President Clinton" as the punch line, but the horndog-in-chief was old news, and Tiger-bashing was all the rage.

There was nothing like a joke to lighten the mood when you were talking about something as serious as cancer, and that was what I was doing all day long.

I'm not complaining; far from it. This was what I went to school to do. Floridians suffered from skin cancer at a rate far above the national average. They call it the Sunshine State after all. My parents and grandparents have had skin cancer, and I knew with what I did in my youth that my turn would come soon; mine and every light-skinned Floridian's.

So despite the greatest recession in thirty years hitting the USA, I was still busy, very busy.

My name is Harold Poe, and I'm a dermatologic surgeon. A dermatologist is an expert on skin diseases and manages many of these problems with the surgical skills that they learn in their training. I seemed to spend all my time treating skin cancer. In fact, I had changed the name of my practice from "Harold Poe, MD - Dermatology" to "The Poe Skin Cancer Center." It seemed hanging out my new shingle was more understandable to the public, i.e. I was the place to go if you had a skin cancer.

***

After finishing with my patient, my new iPhone rang with a ringtone that sounded like an angel's harp, and I quickly answered to hear my wife's voice.

"When will you be done?"

"Probably around 5:00."

"I need you to pick up the kids from school. Amber's lame."

"Sure, honey."

Amber is my wife's horse, and Christina is my wife. The light of my life. Enough bragging.

After I figured out how to hang up my phone, I went to see my next patient.

"Hey, Doc!" Frank smiled, reaching out for my hand and squeezing mine in his ham-fisted grip.

Frank was a cop and a damn good one. We've known each other since high school. He worked Miami Metro. He worked SWAT. And now, he was a full bird homicide detective. That and a healthy application of sunscreen every morning didn't stop the skin cancers from growing on his red-headed skin every time I saw him.

"You've been working out?" Frank's all about the sarcasm.

I puffed up my chest and humbly replied, "Perfection isn't that hard to achieve. Now, have you grown something new?"

"I don't know. That's why I come to see you."

Back to business.

"Sit down and take off your shirt."

I noticed two small crusted scabs over his central chest as I reached out to feel his skin.

"Someone practicing a Taser on you?"

Frank looked at me sideways. "How'd you know that?"

"Can't miss the burns on your chest."

"We can't get certified in their use unless we know what it feels like, so it was finally my turn."

"How'd it feel?"

"Like I was going to piss myself."

"Did you?", I asked noticing a crusted lesion on his head.

"Hell, no."

I gave him the look. Like he couldn't throw a baseball or hammer a nail.

I prepared him for an injection of lidocaine, a local anesthetic.

"You're going to feel a little pinch ..."

While I was performing the biopsy on the non-healing sore on his scalp, Frank hit me with the question that was to change my life.

"Doc, you know a lot about tattoos, don't you?"

3
"Invisible Sun" - The Police

Being a physician was certainly being denigrated these days by the "all-knowing" politicians and bureaucrats in Washington, DC. They were all lawyers, and if there was one thing we learned in medical school, it was that all the law students were jealous of, or at the very least, incompatible with the medical students.

Oh yes, we had many of the rivalries of basketball tournaments between the schools and even some pre-professional mixers, but this rarely led to any real camaraderie. Instead, we developed an uneasy understanding that we doctors were smarter and on the side of angels and, one day, sooner or later, the lawyers were going to get us.

Nationalized healthcare was never about helping the patients; it certainly wasn't about saving money; it was always about lawyers and bureaucrats being in charge of the doctors. Maybe their dreams were dashed in college when they stayed out too late on a drunken bender. They woke up to find they had failed organic chemistry and the dreams of their parents were now ruined. They would never get to be a doctor, so they settled for Plan B - "law school", and they nurtured a smoldering resentment of doctors for the rest of their lives.

Call it karma or one of God's many little ironies, but the sad fact was that my best friend, other than Frank and my wife, was a malpractice attorney. I know what you're thinking that he must be the "good" kind of lawyer who protects doctors from the greedy sons of bitches you see parading their advertisements on the backs of phone books across the nation or whose commercials run every 15 minutes on late night cable television. But you'd be wrong ... dead wrong.

The simple truth is my wife is friends with his wife, and what initially started as only tolerance blossomed into an actual relationship. I considered him far from normal because his thought processes and excuses for his line of work betrayed a poor grasp of morality. However, he did maintain the one virtue that kept us close -- he kept his word.

"Dependability," my mother used to tell me, "is the only real way to judge a true friend."

When I first met Broder I was so uncomfortable I could hardly disguise my distaste for him. I recognized him immediately from his commercials. He only lived two doors down from us and, since Christina and his wife, Hannah, were inseparable, I put on my best face and agreed to have dinner at their home. Broder was ingratiating and talkative. He told me how he had a great understanding of medicine because he had to study the medical literature for each and every client he represented.

"Well, you could almost be considered a doctor then," I offered politely.

"You know the degree we get from law school is called a J.D. for juris doctor, so I'm basically a doctor of law." He puffed up and went to straighten a tie he wasn't wearing.

I nodded feigning interest as he continued.

"You know I always relate well with the doctors I'm suing. It's funny, because I have so much more in common with them than with my clients. These docs are usually young, professional, well-educated, and on the road to starting a family. You know, I really feel sorry for them."

Not being able to swallow anymore of this, I offered a smile. "I'm sure the devil himself has some sympathy for the souls he drags down to hell."

The blood drained out of Broder's cheeks, and I offered him my plate. "Can I have more beef Wellington, please?"

Later, Broder asked me to be an expert witness on one of his cases, and I told him flat out, "I only protect other doctors unless the case is criminal." According to Broder, it was.

Most people have heard about this case. A former soldier in the Cuban army with battlefield "surgical" experience in Angola had entered the United States illegally and decided to present himself to the community as a dermatologist. His practice was mostly directed at the Spanish-only speaking population of Miami and featured his bargain-priced cosmetic services. Cut-rate botox, facial peels, and breast augmentation were his bread and butter. As it was an all cash, up front only, business, none of the insurance companies or state regulating agencies had him on their radar.

A whistleblower nurse thought that his surgical technique was suspect, and she surreptitiously videotaped him using an ice cream scoop as a surgical instrument during a breast enhancement procedure. When it turned out that he wasn't an American citizen, he wasn't licensed, and, of course, he wasn't really a doctor, one of his former patients got Broder involved.

This debacle didn't stop the press from misrepresenting the story and scaring the public with headlines like, "Doctor Used Ice Cream Scoop" and "Patients Thought They Could Trust Their Doctor." Folks, he wasn't a doctor or anything close to one.

Broder brought suit on behalf of several of his victims and got to wear his "white hat" on television for several weeks. For my part, I had the opportunity of teaching Broder a little about dermatology and why it's so much more than acne and Botox. When questioned about my credentials by opposing counsel, they were surprised that I was considered an international expert on skin cancer and skin adornments.

"Skin adornments?" Broder looked intrigued. "like jewelry?"

"Not exactly."

I sat there silently, and stared at Broder and the other attorney. Broder had coached me to answer questions only and to fight the urge to add more to the deposition without questioning.

"Doctors always go into teaching mode, and once they start talking I can sit back and let them give me enough rope to hang them," he told me privately.

The opposing attorney asked the obvious, "What are skin adornments?"

I smiled, "Piercings, cuttings, brandings, implants, and body painting. But most of all, tattoos."

4
"Blister in the Sun" -The Violent Femmes

"I guess I know a little something about tattoos," I answered Frank as I finished his biopsy. "What do you want to know?"

"We have an unusual case, and I just thought you may be able to add something to the investigation."

"Like what?" I asked curiously.

"Sometimes some fresh eyes are helpful. Let me call you after work tonight."

Frank called before my day was finished.

"Let's meet for drinks."

Frank knows I don't drink, but that doesn't stop him from choosing the place.

"How about Hooters?"

Before I could answer, he finished, "Coconut Grove, 5:30? Alright? I'll see you there."

Halfway to Hooters, I realized I had forgotten to pick up the kids from school. Christina would kill me. I called Frank on my new phone, and he picked up on the first ring.

"Hey, buddy."

"Hey Frank, I forgot I'm supposed to pick up the kids right now. Can we do this another time?"

"Sure. No problem, Doc."

***

When I got home with the kids, I was surprised to find that Frank was waiting for me. He had already made himself comfortable in my dining room chair, and Christina smiled as we came in.

"Look who dropped in, Harry." She presented her arm in Frank's direction like she was Vanna White showing a prize car on "Wheel of Fortune". There was a look in her eye meant only for me meaning that she was not happy to have Frank dropping by.

It's not that Christina dislikes Frank; let's just say he wasn't her favorite of my friends. Frank and I go way back from before I met her, and Frank was initially disapproving of our relationship. He regrets what he did, but Christina has never truly forgiven him. After his two marriages ended in failure, Christina can't help but continually point that out as more proof of his bad judgment.

The kids ran over and gave their "Uncle Frank" a big hug. Danielle, our seven-year-old, gave him a kiss on the cheek, and Lizard, our nine-year-old son, tried valiantly to climb on his back. Frank gave a deep rumbling laugh that could only come from smoking too many cigarettes.

We didn't name our only son "Lizard," but it's a nickname that just stuck despite my wife's objections.

"Lizard, you're getting too big," Frank said sarcastically as he lifted him easily off his back.

I noticed the case file on the dining room table and realized Frank must have thought this was very important.

"I thought you were going to Hooters."

The kids giggled. They're young, but they're smart enough to know when grown men were acting foolishly. I asked Christina to watch the kids while I spoke to Frank privately. I knew I was going to hear about the Hooters comment but she nodded. I walked with Frank into the living room.

5
"No More Sunshine" - Kevin Quain & the Mad Bastards

Frank began.

"Yesterday, we were called to an apartment on South Beach where a 22-year-old woman was found dead. She had bled out from every orifice - her mouth, nose, ears, vagina and anus ... even her eyes."

"Had she traveled recently?" I asked.

"Why do you ask that?"

"Well, hemorrhagic fever initially comes to mind."

"Hemorrhagic fever?"

"You ever heard of Ebola virus?"

"Holy shit! No one ever considered that."

"Really?" I asked incredulously.

"No, Sherlock. We had the Hazmat team down there, and all that stuff was negative. We know what killed her ... she was poisoned."

"Warfarin?"

"It looks like all that money your parents spent to send you to medical school wasn't wasted."

"Jeez, Frank, I thought you wanted my help. I don't see what you need me for if you already have all the answers."

"We know how she died, but we don't know why. This girl was a beautiful fashion model with everything going for her." Frank fumbled through the file in front of him. "It's such a waste. We have to know why someone would mutilate her."

"Mutilate her?" I asked.

"Uh-huh. Here are some pictures of her work."

He handed me a portfolio of modeling photos and print ads which showed off the victim's exceptionally good looks. Frank pointed at one provocatively posed 8 by 10. I was immediately aware of my heart pounding because the victim eerily resembled what I imagined my daughter

Danielle would look like when she was all grown up. I muttered a silent prayer for this girl and felt a twinge of guilt about being thankful she was someone else's daughter.

"Notice the lower back?"

"Yes."

"See the tattoo?"

"Of course."

"What can you tell me?"

I stared at the photograph. At the base of her spine was a tiny tattoo of a horse. The design was distinctive. It was outlined in black with an unusual white ink coloring the body of the horse. It was running to the right, but looking backwards over its shoulder. I recognized something about the design and looked into Frank's questioning eyes. I answered with one word.

"Venezuela."

6
"Here Comes the Sun" - The Beatles

My life changed when I got into medical school, and I haven't had time to look back. We learned a bit of everything about medicine when we were in school. Besides striving to dazzle the professors with our brilliance, we quickly learned that we were at the bottom of the barrel and shit flowed downhill. Now this saying was heard often, but in medicine it was literal. Ask anybody outside of medicine if they ever had to dis-impact a constipated patient to find out the truth.

The med students became "scut monkeys" for the interns and residents who were like the junior doctors. A bad word from them whispered into the ear of a professor could spell an end to a dream residency appointment. Taking care of patients never seemed so daunting.

Part of my many requirements for graduation was to do three months of Family Medicine for my fourth year. This requirement was put in place because the medical schools had been mandated by the government to direct more students into "primary care" and away from the specialties. This requirement effectively used up our valuable elective time. This was all well and good if I wanted to be a family practitioner but if I wanted to be a surgeon, a urologist, or a dermatologist, this took away my opportunities to do a visiting rotation at another school in the specialty I was pursuing.

I figured if I had to do primary care, I wanted to make sure it was a memorable learning experience. Christina found out about an opportunity for me to do a primary care rotation outside of the country in Venezuela through the Catholic Medical Mission Board. The dean of the medical school, Dr. Hawthorne, was uneasy about letting me go abroad, but he admired what he called my "adventurous spirit," and he signed off.

Christina and I flew south from Miami and started a month-long adventure we'd never forget. We landed in the capital, Caracas, where we quickly hopped a small propeller plane to Canaima and began an eight hour journey through the Guiana highlands.

Whenever faced with the choice to take a first class ticket on a bus ride in Latin America or a second class ticket, my advice is pay the few dollars more for first class. Christina and I were on a budget, and we took second class. Big mistake.

At first everything was fine when we got on the bus in Canaima camp, a quaint village that tourists frequent to visit Venezuela's wondrous Angel Falls. Christina sat on a seat, and we stowed our luggage between us. On the way, the bus made a multitude of stops, and every time more people got on the bus. The traditional rainments of the Pemon Indians were interesting and the things they carried even more so -- machetes, boxes of fruit, and live chickens. Within thirty minutes the bus was so crowded I found myself snuggled into the armpit of an elderly gentlemen whose last bath must have been when the Spaniards still held dominion over this beautiful country.

The sights and smells of the bus ride were bad enough, but the humidity and heat made it next to unbearable. At one point in our long journey, I nodded off and was uncomfortably awakened when our bus nearly slammed into a van. The packed passengers readjusted themselves, and a few prayers were said but other than that it was treated as a normal event.

It was night when we arrived in Santa Elena de Uairén, a small city near the borders with Brazil and Guayana. As we entered the church, we were met by Father Lorenzo, an American priest who had been working with the Pemon Indians for fifteen years. He was warm and welcoming and was even more excited when we produced a bottle of Maker's Mark bourbon from the duty-free in Miami. His arm was in a splint from a recent fall and, when I offered to examine him, he assured me that he was alright.

Christina gave the priest a big hug and told him, "I'm so glad we're finally here."

Father Lorenzo smiled. "Oh no, you still have to get up to Manakrü."

I gave Father Lorenzo a blank look.

"Doctor Marcos' clinic is in Manakrü. That's about a two hour drive straight up the mountains."

He introduced us to Sister San Juana who was waiting to drive us up. She was a young, strong woman who wore a habit of white that miraculously remained spotless despite the muddy roads we walked on.

When she led us to her pick-up truck, we found about fifteen men sitting in its bed awaiting our arrival. Sister San Juana said something to them in an Indian dialect, and they all smiled at us. They took our luggage onto the truck, and Sister San Juana asked Christina to sit in the cab. I jumped into the bed of the crowded truck with the rest of the men.

I noticed that they all carried machetes. A friendly Spanish-speaking man introduced himself as Emeliano, "We are thankful that you've come to help us, el doctor."

I smiled, thanked him, and couldn't quite get used to being called "el doctor" as I thought of myself as only a fourth year student. I was trained at school not to refer to myself as a doctor until I had earned it.

"I heard you are from Florida, el doctor. *Verdad*?" he asked. A statement in Spanish can be quickly changed into a question by adding "*verdad*" which basically means truth or "is that true?"

"Yes, I live in Miami," I replied.

The other men who spoke only the indigenous dialect seemed to understand the name Miami and I heard them whisper it to each other reverentially.

"Oh, el doctor, I dream that one day I will go to Miami. Maybe I can visit you."

"That would be great!" I offered.

Two hours of bumps, ruts, mud, and holes later and we entered the indigenous village of Manakrü. It was so dark that I could make out little of its characteristics.

Many times we would stop and let one of the men off the truck. Each time they would leave Emeliano would mutter "*Adiós, hermano.*" One time instead of his usual goodbye, Emeliano said "*Adiós, cabrón!*" and a fight ensued as the remaining men punched and beat the man as he was trying to get out of the truck. The young man who was the victim of the beating fell out onto the dirt road with a thud and then quickly picked himself up and ran off into the darkness.

"What are you doing?" I asked Emeliano.

Emeliano smiled as he tried to reassure me, but I found his expression to be unnerving instead. "It is nothing, el doctor. You do not yet understand our ways, but you will."

I figured this must be some type of hazing ritual, and I became wary of when my turn to leave the truck arrived.

The clinic was one of the few lighted buildings we saw. The remaining men on the truck quickly hopped out and silently dispersed into the darkness. Sister San Juana brought us into the walls of the clinic compound, and we were met by Doctor Marcos. He was an older man who had the face of a boxer. His nose had been broken and had healed at a funny angle. He smiled as we came in.

He actually ogled Christina a little, then gave her a big hug. Then he grasped my hand firmly in his and told me in perfect English, "Doctor Poe, I'm so glad you're here. I'll be away for two weeks tending the sick in Vila Brasil, and we'll need you to run the clinic while I'm gone."

7
"Seasons in the Sun" - Terry Jacks

"Venezuela? What do you mean?" Frank narrowed his eyes.

"Yes," I told him. "That horse is a distinctive part of the Venezuelan coat of arms. Is she ... was she Venezuelan?"

"No, she was an American of Cuban descent."

The term "Cuban-American" was no longer politically correct as most of their community emphasized their loyalty to America first.

"You mentioned that she was mutilated."

Frank produced a coroner's report, and showed me another photograph. The victim's lower back had been cut in a large rectangle, and her skin and tattoo had been peeled off.

"Grisly," I whispered.

"The skin wasn't recovered. We figure we have a trophy hunter."

"Sick. But I don't think that's the right way."

"The right way?"

"The right way of thinking. Frank, can we still examine the body?"

Frank rolled his shoulders. "Yes, but you won't see anything not documented in this report. They're extremely thorough."

"Let's stop at my office on the way. I need to pick something up."

***

The coroner's office of Dade County isn't a warm fuzzy place. It is a large rectangular building, and it has all the architectural grandeur that the government could muster in the 1970's. They tried their best to make it inviting, but it's hard to sugarcoat a bitter pill. The first thing you notice is that the air-conditioner works too well. It's cold.

The ghoul working the night shift smiled widely as we walked through the door marked "Morgue." "Detective Martin, to what do I deserve this honor?"

"Shut up, Coltrane, I want to introduce you to my dermatologist, Doctor Harold Poe."

"Your personal dermatologist?" Coltrane looked over his glasses. "Have you gone Hollywood, Detective?" He shook my hand. "You gonna give him a facial, Doc? If so I want to help because we don't often get to see living patients down here or many as ugly as Frank here."

"Are you saying Frank is living?" I offered.

"Large, boys. Living large," Frank kicked in and was obviously and quickly getting to the point where the kidding stopped.

Coltrane smiled. "What can I do for you gentlemen at this hour?"

Frank's face took on the business as usual look that cops master within a year. "We want to look at Lourdes Rivera."

Coltrane led us into the locker room and presented her remains to us. "She was a pretty girl, Frank, but I think she's well past the need of a dermatologist."

Frank looked at me as I opened my bag to produce a Wood's lamp.

"What are you looking for, Doc?"

A Wood's lamp was a tool dermatologists used to observe fluorescent skin diseases like erythrasma or to dilineate depigmentation from conditions like vitiligo. It was basically a "black light" similar to those used by hippies to illuminate psychedelic posters and by dance clubs across the world.

I was looking for "rave tattoos." I took the hand-held light out and asked Coltrane to turn down the lights.

"Doc, we use Wood's lamps, too. We didn't find anything worth noting."

"Please turn down the lights," I insisted.

Coltrane flicked a switch, and the room became completely dark. I turned on the Wood's lamp, and a few things became apparent.

One was that Miss Rivera's body had a fine covering of lint. Two was Frank's white shirt had a stain on it that I didn't see before, and three, Coltrane needed to see a dentist.

I moved the lamp over her prone body and spent time looking at the wound at the small of her back. Something about the white color of her horse tattoo had made me consider that it might have been a fluorescent ink. Fluorescent inks were used in the so-called "rave" tattoos because they were meant to light up on the dance floor when seen under the lights at night clubs. When seen in normal light they aren't as impressive, and the white inks sometimes appeared chalky. I didn't find any sign of fluorescence at her wound.

I moved to put the lamp away when I noticed something bright on her left ring finger.

"Frank, look at this."

Where many wear a wedding band, there was instead a bright smear of whiteness. On closer inspection, the smear was reminiscent of a map of the island of Cuba tattooed on her skin.

Frank asked Coltrane to turn on the lights. When he did, the tattoo disappeared.

"What the ..." Frank reacted with astonishment. "Coltrane, turn the lights off again."

He did, and the tattoo blazed in all its fluorescent glory. I told Coltrane to turn the light back on.

"Doc, what do you make of that?" he asked.

"Let me have some gloves, please," I requested.

I slipped on a pair of latex examination gloves and motioned to Coltrane to look at what I was doing. I gently felt the buttocks of the victim, and my suspicions were rewarded. I started to massage them, pushing the tissues upward toward the wound on her back. Frank gave me an odd look until he and Coltrane noticed the oily substance extruding from the wound.

"Mr. Coltrane, you need to get a sample of this fluid, and we need to do some biopsies of her buttocks."

8
"Why Does the Sun Shine?" - They
Might Be Giants

"I've never seen a tattoo like that. First, there's nothing there, and then blam! It's bright as a light bulb. I take it you've seen them before."

I nodded as I stuffed the last bit of my patty melt sandwich into my mouth. We had stopped at Friendly's in Coconut Grove to get a "treat," as Frank liked to say.

I first heard about fluorescent or "rave" tattoos when I was a guest speaker at the South Florida Tattoo Convention. One of the artists asked me a question about the safety of fluorescent tattoos. The primary manufacturer of the ink was called Crazy Chameleon and, according to their proprietary information, it had been used safely to mark fish for many years. Not completely comfortable with fish testing, I basically told her that I couldn't answer her question, but I wondered aloud if the fluorescent energy would cause itching or irritation in the skin. She told me that the most popular ink was a skin-colored variety that, once healed, was virtually invisible.

The tattoo artist needed to wear a special lighted headpiece that shined the black light onto the skin during the application procedure so that the extent of the fluorescent ink could be seen.

This invisible tattoo appeared to be all the rage of club-goers and working professionals who sought to avoid the stigma of their tattoo on the job but enjoyed the thrill of it when on the dance floor.

"Do you think there are any particular tattoo parlors who use that ink?" Frank asked.

"It's gotten pretty common. Artists might recognize the horse design, though. I'd be more interested in the silicone."

"Is that what that was?"

"I think so, but I would still wait for the lab results. If it is silicone, that would be a genuine lead."

"How so?" Frank remained interested.

"Depending on the grade of silicone used, you should be able to narrow down where she had the procedure done."

I wiped my hands on my napkin and continued, "Industrial grade silicone is used by amateurs at events called pumping parties. These are commonplace in the transsexual community. Higher grade silicone is used by few reputable physicians. Plastic surgeons and dermatologists could use it, but most find it problematic because the silicone can travel far from where it was injected."

Then it hit me.

"Another thing to think of is scalpel tourism. Frank, I should have thought of this immediately. Because of the recession, a lot of people are bargain shopping for plastic surgery, and they're willing to travel outside the country to get it. It doesn't hurt that the destination is a tropical paradise where their recovery from surgery is truly like a dream vacation."

Frank smiled, "A trip to the Caribbean and you come home with great tits or a J Lo-style ass."

"Exactly. And the number one destination for these low-priced lifts is none other than Venezuela."

9
"When The Sun Goes Down" - Kenny
Chesney & Uncle Kracker

When I got home, Christina and the kids
were already asleep. I slipped into the bed
next to Christina and was just making
myself comfortable cuddling up to her when
the bed shifted and groaned. Little Pinch
pushed her way between us and wiggled
onto her back, then her tail thumped the
mattress as she wagged it expectantly.

I reached over and patted her belly
happily. Little Pinch isn't little. She's a
rescued dog that Christina got from the
pound as a puppy. She'd been abused by her
previous owners. They had leashed a noose

around her neck which had crushed her throat and damaged her vocal cords so badly that she couldn't bark anymore. The people at the pound told us she was "mostly pit bull with just a little pinscher." I fell in love with her immediately and, since every time I inject a patient with a needle I tell them they're going to feel a "little pinch," I felt her name was destiny.

When I was a dermatology resident, I told a VA patient that he was going to feel a "little prick" when I injected him with anesthetic. He quickly replied, "That's what your wife felt on your honeymoon, a little prick!" I now used the term "little pinch" exclusively, and it always reminded me of our beloved pooch.

She was a big girl now. She weighed 110 pounds and was still growing. She had black and white fur that looked like a Holstein cow. She was good with the kids and Christina, but she was most attentive to me.

When we first got her, she was so frightened of me that she would piss all over the place, then roll on her back and continue wetting herself. As she learned to trust me and got more comfortable with us, she stopped soiling herself except at rare times when she was really excited. It was always somewhat disquieting as she would try to bark, but nothing would ever come out, not a peep. But Christina said that she could still communicate volumes with just one look from her big beautiful brown eyes.

As I lay there rubbing Little Pinch's furry belly, I couldn't stop thinking about Lourdes Rivera, fluorescent tattoos, silicone injections, and most of all, Venezuela.

10
"Sun is Shining" - Bob Marley & the Wailers

Working the clinic alone with no supervision was daunting. Christina loved to roam the town with the Sisters, and she would help them prepare all the meals at the "*clinica.*" I was incredibly nervous and couldn't wait for Dr. Marcos' return.

All morning we would see patients, and they were expected to pay something for our services. Whether it was a live chicken which the Sisters would quickly dispatch and prepare for dinner or fresh vegetables from their gardens, this type of bartering was encouraged. Rarely, the people would pay money to the Sisters. Sister San Juana told me matter-of-factly that the clinic was charitable and would always treat the sick even if they were too poor to pay, but the people needed to maintain their self-respect. We afforded them the dignity to pay what they could. In their culture, no one wanted to be considered "useless" or lazy, so they were expected to pay something.

Many mornings there would be sixty to seventy people waiting for the clinic to start at 7:00 a.m., and they would have with them a menagerie of poultry and a cornucopia of fruits, vegetables, and baked goods. The most common problems we dealt with were traumatic injuries and their subsequent infections. We had a "*farmacia*" stocked with out-of-date and expired antibiotics, but Sister San Juana always reminded us that "God provides." The medicines of the pharmacy were mostly donated from the Catholic mission and churches. Most of the medicine was clearly from the United States, but others were labeled in Spanish, French, and Portuguese. This made it quite difficult for me to recognize what the medicines even were as I struggled to know how to use those I knew.

Every day a lunch was prepared at noon, and it usually consisted of chicken, rice, beans and "*pan*," or bread. They always served this with a wonderful hot cup of coffee, which was fine with Christina and me as we were warned not to drink the water.

Lunch began with a prayer and ended with a portion of the Rosary. It was wonderful to hear the prayers I knew so well in English recited in Spanish. Then Sister San Juana and I would round on the "in-patients" who were so sick that they stayed at the clinic. The ward was made up of six beds. The patients would rest on their bed, and many times their families would set up camp beneath the bed.

One of the patients was a ten-year-old boy named Leal who was diagnosed by Dr. Marcos as having encephalitis. He had presented in a coma a week prior to Christina's and my arrival at the compound. We treated him with broad spectrum antibiotics and hoped he would recover. While his treatment was truly basic and the facilities were spare, the care he received from the nuns was touching. The Sisters would clean his diaper every three hours and bathe and swaddle him with such love. We struggled to feed him, and Christina helped with his diet, using the skills she learned as a nutrition major in college.

After rounding on the in-patients, we'd walk past the brutish watchdog named Ursus who guarded the front of the clinic compound. He never had a problem with Christina or any woman for that matter, but he hated all men and me in particular. Getting past him was difficult as I would have to walk around the farthest expanse of his leash with him barking and trying to bite me.

The Sisters thought this was hilarious. Once I got around Ursus, the Sisters would re-open the large heavy doors of the clinic compound, and I would begin to see the new mass of people waiting for us.

The Pemon Indians made up the majority of the population we served, and they were a short people. In fact, Christina and I towered over them. The term "Pemon" actually means "The People". This translation led me to misread an important conversation I was to have.

I had just seen a young man named Junio with a large, firm mass in his right scrotum who most certainly had testicular cancer. He was going to need radiation therapy, and that was certainly not available in Manakrü. According to Sister San Juana, the nearest hospital was 300 miles away in Ciudad Bolívar. We talked to Junio and his wife about travel, and they looked like we had asked them to go to the moon. They had no car and little money. Sister San Juana told them that if they could get down to see Father Lorenzo in Santa Elena de Uairén that he would find a way to get them to the hospital.

As we were saying goodbye to Junio, I looked up at the waiting line of patients and noticed a disruption in the crowd as a man pushed his way through. Behind him came a man holding a bloody rag over his left forearm. I quickly recognized the leader as Emeliano, the man I had met in the truck on the ride up the mountains to Manakrü.

"El doctor!" he shouted with a large toothy smile. I noticed the crowd backed away from him and made way for the bloodied man behind him. "You must help this man. He's been cut very badly."

I led them into the examining room and asked the injured man to lie down.

"El doctor, my man, Javíer, was hit with a machete." When Emeliano pronounced his friend's name, the "r" at the end rolled off his tongue like the purr of a lion.

I unwrapped Javíer's bandages and exposed a six inch laceration over his anterior forearm, and arterial blood shot out onto my shirt. I replaced the bandage with pressure.

Sister San Juana was ready with a lidocaine syringe and a surgical kit with suture. I tried to anesthetize the skin around the forearm wound while San Juana maintained pressure on the site.

Once the wound was numb, I had San Juana pull the bandage back to expose the artery. Moving quickly, I encircled the cut blood vessel with a loop of suture and just as swiftly tied it off. Sister San Juana cut the suture, and I repeated the looping of the artery farther down from the cut. Once the blood had stopped pumping, we set to work cleaning the wound, repairing the tissues, and closing the skin.

Emeliano had kept quiet throughout the procedure, but as we were finishing up, he became more talkative.

"El doctor, you did a wonderful thing!"

I smiled and, for one of the few moments since I took over the clinic, I felt a sense of accomplishment.

"Thank you, Emeliano."

"No, thank you, el doctor." Something changed in the set of his eyes as he became more excited. "You could do so much more, el doctor."

"What do you mean?" I wondered aloud.

"A rich American like you could give some money for the people."

"The Pemon?" I asked, trying to understand and hopefully avoid confrontation.

"Of course," he smiled and added, "and the people's movement."

"Well, I didn't bring a lot of money with me on this trip."

"It wouldn't be a lot of money for you, my friend. Let's say 500 dollars."

I laughed and noticed out of the corner of my eye that Sister San Juana looked extremely nervous.

"No worries, Emeliano." I smiled, too. "But this is the first time someone has asked me to pay after I provided the service to them."

Emeliano was no longer smiling. "We'll come back to this, el doctor." He waved a hand at his man. "Let's go, Javíer!"

And just like that they left the room and marched away from the clinic as the rest of the patients moved quickly to get out of their way.

11
"Let the Sunshine In" - The 5th Dimension

Melanoma skin cancer is one of the worst diagnoses I deal with in my practice, and it also takes a significant amount of time to counsel a melanoma patient about their proper care. I had been talking to a 19-year-old girl about her biopsy which showed a particularly deep melanoma. Her parents and boyfriend were with her, and everyone was hoping for answers and were decidedly terrified. I recommended my colleague, Dr. Loewinger, who would perform a procedure called the sentinel node biopsy to see if the cancer had spread to her lymph nodes.

Her mother grabbed my hand and asked, "Why did this happen to my daughter?

I held her hand tightly and told them again, "As I mentioned before, we blame the development of melanoma on sun exposure and many link it to severe sunburning."

Her mother continued, "Doctor, our daughter has been tanning in our salon. I mean ... we own a tanning salon. That's safe, isn't it?"

A recent national report had shown a spike in the incidence of malignant melanomas in young women. This increase had been linked to the women's use of tanning beds. This had also been a long-term advocacy issue for dermatologists as all skin cancer rates go up with increased exposure to ultraviolet radiation. The reasons why anyone would pay for more ultraviolet light exposure while living in Miami was beyond my imagination.

"We're actually very worried about tanning beds, Mrs. King. Do you offer airbrushing or bronzing?"

She nodded her head. "Yes, we do."

"Good. Most responsible tanning salons offer those services and, now that this experience has hit so close to home, I would recommend moving the bulk of your business toward that."

Sunless tanners had taken off, and dermatologists agree that it's much safer than UV. The successful salons that make it work offer airbrushing application, and many women and girls get this done prior to dances, homecoming, prom, and wedding parties. I couldn't think of a better job for a teenage boy. I would have to have Christina remind me of that when Lizard got older.

I knew I was getting behind, so I made sure everyone knew that the next step was to see Dr. Loewinger and that I would see them again after the surgery. I left my nurse Carmencita with them to give them some educational pamphlets, and I said my goodbyes and moved quickly down the hall to my next patient.

Knowing enough to preemptively prevent complaints when running late, I began apologizing before I even entered the next examination room.

"I'm so sorry to keep you waiting."

I looked at the examination table and was met with a big smile from "Sweet Pete" Underwood. Pete had been my patient for years and always was a bright part of any day that I saw him. HIV positive since the 80's, Pete was a walking, talking medical miracle of survival.

I first met him at Jackson Memorial Hospital when I was still just a resident in training. We had little to offer AIDS patients in those days except an antiviral called AZT and prophylactic antibiotics to prevent expected diseases as their immune systems deteriorated. Sweet Pete was initially a psoriasis patient and, tiring of topical creams and lotions, he would self-treat with sun tanning via prolonged visits to the local nudist beach, Haulover.

Despite my objections, Pete would show up at the clinic in all his 300 pound glory with a full body tan of a deep coffee brown. I told him he'd get skin cancer, and eventually he did. But at the time he had more important things to worry about, like a worsening immune system and little hope for the future.

As part of this realization, Sweet Pete lived every moment like it was his last, and he vowed to never say anything bad about anyone. Hence the moniker "Sweet" had less to do with his sexual orientation than it did with his eternal optimism and overt charming disposition.

An interesting addition to his vow of living life to the fullest, "Sweet Pete" was active in the tattoo and body piercing subculture which had begun to flourish in the newly renovated ghettos of South Beach. He had lots of tattoos and lots of piercings.

A remarkable tattoo over his left shoulder was a large biohazard symbol that read within it "HIV positive." This was not only a warning to his potential partners, but his sign of solidarity with the infected. During the years of my training, we lost countless numbers of patients to this dreaded disease. They would die from an unbelievable variety of infections that would only affect human beings who had lost their immune defenses.

Things changed when the "cocktail" was invented. New antiviral medicines called protease inhibitors forever changed the landscape of HIV treatment and offered the possibility of a normal life span to the infected. What didn't change was Sweet Pete's attitude. Ever the positive force and eternal optimist, he sat before me awaiting my examination.

"Sweet Pete."

"How you doing, Doc?"

"Great!"

I looked him over. Pete was in great shape. When I first met him he was a big fat tub of guts, but as he got into the tattoo scene, he also started working out. He was a muscle-bound 250 pound bad-ass who had enough tattoo ink and skin jewelry to intimidate most people. In fact, many of my patients upon seeing him would have run out of my waiting room if he didn't have a certain smile and a special way that let you know immediately that he was harmless. I've never seen him mad and I would never want to. It would ruin our wonderful world.

Patients always ask if there's a link between tattoos and skin cancer, and the answer is not simple. The exhibitionism that goes along with showing off a tattoo often is associated with greater sun exposure. If there's no greater sun exposure, than my opinion would be that there's no link.

I was examining Sweet Pete's arm when I noticed a white tattoo and was reminded of poor Lourdes Rivera.

"Hey Pete, is this tattoo fluorescent?"

"Yeah, Doc. I've got a few of them. You should see me on the dance floor at night. I light up like a Christmas tree."

I smiled and asked my assistant Cammy for my prescription pad. I tried my best to draw the Venezuelan horse design. Then I held it up for Sweet Pete. "Have you ever seen a tattoo like this one?"

12
"Tequila Sunrise" - The Eagles

Erzulie Murphy is an artist and a real talented one. Originally from Haiti, her family fled to Miami to escape the political violence of that poor country. It is truly the poorest nation in the New World (with Cuba running a close second) but it is rich with the artistic talent of its people. It is said that there are more talented artists per square foot of land in Haiti than anywhere else in the world.

Erzulie grew up in Miami and went to art school in Savannah. There she won many awards, and her paintings were noted to show striking emotional design flourishes. Her subjects were so meticulously detailed that many believed she was taking photographs. All her professors agreed that her artistic skills were extraordinary. She could be a fine artist exhibiting in museums and selling her works at the finest galleries in the world but that was not her desire or passion. She liked to use her gifts making tattoos.

I first met Erzulie when I was invited to speak at the South Florida Tattoo Convention a few years ago, and she sat in the very front row for my lecture on the medical considerations of tattoos, body piercings, and other skin adornments. Good tattoo artists are always interested in improving their skills and abilities so that they can avoid problems for their clients. She struck me as bright and highly motivated, and I only found out later about her artistic skills. She built a strong reputation for herself in a tough market dominated by male tattoo artists. Part of her marketing plan included the establishment of a female-artist-only tattoo convention which was currently celebrating its third anniversary.

Sweet Pete had told me that her "Tattoo Girl Power" convention was this weekend and that I needed to go talk to Erzulie. "If anyone would recognize that tattoo it would be Erzulie," Pete said. "And her show begins tonight at the Delano."

Frank was up for a "field trip" as he called it and we drove to the Delano on Miami Beach after work. The Delano seemed like an unlikely place for a tattoo convention as it was very expensive and very upscale. This was where the celebrities stayed when they flocked to South Beach.

"Are they going to let us in?" Frank asked.

"Of course," I answered as we were getting out of our car and I handed my keys to the valet. "Why wouldn't they?"

"I thought it was only for women," he explained.

"No, it's only for female artists, but the customers can be of any gender. Do you want to get a tattoo?"

"Harry, I'm on duty. You can get one for the both of us."

We walked into the entrance of the hotel and followed the signs directing us to the show. The convention area was a large meeting hall with anywhere from thirty to thirty-five booths each decorated with large banners promoting the names of the individual tattoo studios and the artists representing them. One particular banner caught my eye which featured a provocative illustration of a partially dressed woman with a script covering her private areas that read "Man's Ruin".

As we made our way through the line to the registration table I checked my wallet to see if I had enough cash. The entrance fee turned out to be fifty bucks each. Maybe that was how they afforded the Delano.

I stepped up to the table and smiled at the two young women guarding the entrance. One had a blonde Mohawk with pink highlights at the tips of her remaining hairs. She had her nose and lower lip pierced, and her left arm was completely tattooed or "sleeved up". The girl next to her was buxom. She had a full head of black hair with her bangs cut across her forehead like Bettie Page and she was dressed like a pin-up from the 1950's right down to the fishnet stockings and high heels.

"I'd like two tickets," I said holding out a hundred dollars to Mohawk who was operating the money box.

She looked over at Bettie Page and then back at me and said "It's not that simple, mister."

I'm sure I looked confused.

"Show us your tattoo or you can't go in," Mohawk said matter-of-factly.

"I don't have any tattoos," I replied.

"Sorry, sailor," the Bettie Page look-alike interjected. "Show rules are that no one gets in unless they are part of the people."

"What if we came to get a tattoo?" Frank added while smiling at Bettie.

"This isn't the place to get your first tattoo, sweetie," Mohawk said, and there wasn't anything sweet about her tone. "We are trying to keep the creeps and gawkers to a minimum at this show, so if you don't have a tattoo we can't let you in."

Implicit in her use of the words "creeps" and "gawkers" was the accusation that that was what we were and I could feel the red sting of embarrassment filling my face. Just as we were going to tuck our tails under and leave in disgrace, a voice from the convention hall called out.

"He has a tattoo!" Erzulie Murphy stuck her head through the doorway and smiled. She casually brushed her dreadlocks from her forehead and held out her right hand. "Show her your middle finger, Doc."

I looked at Frank and then at Mohawk and held up the middle finger of my right hand in a gesture that is found uniformly offensive.

Mohawk wasn't smiling. "Erzulie, I don't see anything."

"Look near his fingernail," Erzulie said.

Mohawk and Bettie grabbed my finger and noticed the small black dot next to my fingernail. Bettie looked unimpressed.

"I don't get it," said Mohawk looking back at Erzulie.

"It's a graphite tattoo," she said. "It's a common type of traumatic tattoo from a pencil injury."

I guess Erzulie had been listening during my lecture and remembered me showing off the graphite tattoo. It remained a reminder of my childhood when my sister had accidentally poked me with a pencil.

"Come on. Really?" Mohawk said with all the biting sarcasm she could muster.

Erzulie laughed and motioned toward the ladies who were now laughing too. "Randy and Kale I'd like you to meet Doctor Harry Poe."

They smiled and Mohawk said "Erzulie saw you come in and told us to give you a hard time. Our show is open to anyone who pays, and no one needs a tattoo to get into the show ... but we'd be happy to get you something better than that pencil mark."

I introduced Frank to Erzulie, and we left Randy and Kale as we entered the showroom. The sound of the electric tattoo guns at each booth made a buzzing that reminded me of a beehive, and the queen bee of the event was Erzulie. As we walked past all the booths it was as if we were in the company of royalty. The lady artists who manned the booths would stop what they were doing to nod reverently to Erzulie, and a few would brush their hands against her hand and react electrically to her touch.

Erzulie wore a black bikini top beneath a sheer forest green tunic that included a matching collar of green feathers that looked like it was part of a showgirl's feather boa. Her short skirt was of black leather, and her outfit was finished off with thigh high leather boots of the same forest green. There were tiny green feathers and ribbons at the end of each of her dreadlocks that seemed to accentuate her wondrous green eyes. Her skin could be described as cafe au lait or coffee with cream, and her brown skin in the forest green outfit gave me the impression of being in the presence of a magical woodland faerie.

Erzulie's right arm was completely "sleeved up" and an image of a Rosary ending with a crucifix stood out prominently on her right shoulder. I noted that some of the female artists that touched her shoulder as we walked by immediately crossed themselves in the Catholic tradition.

The finest and most opulent of the tattoo booths had a banner that read "Girl Power Studios featuring Erzulie Murphy", and the decorations included imagery from Christianity mixed with Haitian vevers or symbols from Voodoo. As we approached several women quickly got up from a large green leather recliner and a matching love seat.

"Do you need anything, Erzulie?" asked one of the women.

Erzulie smiled and pointed at Frank and me. "Chelsea, these are my friends Frank and Doctor Poe."

"Hi," Chelsea said. "Would you guys like something to drink?"

"What've you got?" Frank asked.

"We were just planning to mix up some cocktails," Chelsea said excitedly. "Would you like a Mojito?"

"That would be awesome," Frank said with a smile.

"None for me. I don't drink." I added.

"That's too bad," Chelsea said with what sounded like sincere sympathy. "Can I get you a Coke?"

"That would be great."

Chelsea left us, and Erzulie sat down on the green leather recliner. I looked over at Frank as we sat down on the love seat.

"I thought you were on duty."

Frank checked his watch. "It's 7:12 pm, and I am officially off the clock."

Chelsea returned immediately with a Coke for me and three tall glasses of golden liquid with crushed ice that were each decorated with a sprig of fresh mint leaves and a stirring stick made of sliced sugar cane.

Chelsea served Frank and Erzulie first and then grabbed the last glass for herself and squeezed herself between Frank and me on the loveseat. She clinked her glass with Frank's and with a smile said "Cheers."

Frank said, "Thanks," and took a sip. His face noticeably brightened and he complimented Chelsea. "This is a fantastic drink."

Erzulie leaned forward and clinked her glass against my Coke and said, "So Doctor Poe, what brings you and the policeman here on a Friday night to see me?"

I was stunned that Erzulie knew that Frank was police as he wore no uniform, only a Hawaiian shirt and slacks, and I wondered if she had met him before. The only clue to his job might be the small gun in his ankle holster which was hard to notice with his long pants. In Florida, it was very easy to get a concealed weapons permit, and so just having a firearm wouldn't mean someone was necessarily police. Counter-intuitively the states that issued concealed weapons permits had drastically lower crime rates, and gun advocates would tell you that an armed populace was a safer populace.

I looked at Erzulie and figured the direct approach would be best. "Frank is investigating a murder victim who had a distinctive tattoo, and Sweet Pete told me you would be the most helpful in recognizing it."

"I'll certainly try to help. How is Peter?" she asked.

"He's doing great," I replied.

I looked over to Frank to have him join in the discussion and found that he and Chelsea were engaged in a conversation of their own.

"Hey Frank, can you show Erzulie the photos?" I interrupted.

Frank turned his gaze from Chelsea and looked a little disoriented, and then he raised his glass toward me.

"Sorry Doc, this isn't a standard Mojito. It's an exceptional drink, but I tasted Rhum Barbancourt and I wanted to have Chelsea give me her recipe."

Erzulie smiled widely. "The detective has an expertise in cocktails."

Frank, ever humble, produced the pictures of Lourdes Rivera's horse tattoo and said, "I don't consider myself an expert but certainly a cocktail enthusiast."

He passed the photos to Erzulie. She took a deep sip of her drink and set the tall glass down on the end table between her recliner and the love seat. She picked up the photos and sat back, propping her feet up on the extended footrest.

"I didn't make this tattoo, but it is excellent work. I can sometimes recognize a particular artist by his or her work, but I'm not seeing that. I do find something familiar about it though. Let me think."

Erzulie leaned forward and took another deep sip of her Mojito, and then sat back in her big comfy recliner and lifted her legs onto the left arm of the chair. I noticed the steel toe reinforcement on the tips of her boots. She flipped through the pictures a few times and then sat back up straight in the chair and leaned forward toward me, Frank, and Chelsea.

"It's going to come to me. There is something familiar about that tattoo. I'm sure of that," she said.

My new cell phone made a beeping sound, and I pulled it from my pocket. I had received a text. It was from Christina and it read: Dinner in 30 minutes. It was followed by two symbols "<3" and ":)". She was better at this stuff than I was. I looked back at Erzulie and said, "Well, if you remember anything can you call me?"

"Of course, Doctor Poe. I wonder if you wouldn't mind looking at Chelsea. She has a problem with her navel piercing."

"No problem," I said and turned toward Chelsea who was lifting her blouse to show us her belly ring. Frank leaned in for a closer look, and Chelsea giggled.

"Let the doctor take a look, silly," she scolded Frank.

I noticed some redness where the jewelry entered her skin and there was some flaking around the periphery of the rash. There are really three common problems for non-healing belly button piercings. The first is allergy to the jewelry if it contains nickel but hers looked like gold. The second is allergy to something applied to the wound like Neosporin or triple antibiotic cream.

"Have you applied any creams to the wound?" I asked with my doctor's mind taking over.

"No," she said.

That left the more unusual third cause -- an unrecognized yeast infection.

"Try over-the-counter Monistat cream twice a day, and that should fix you up," I offered. Chelsea thanked me profusely, and I stood up to face Erzulie.

I thanked her again and noticed that many of the booths were closing down and that the buzz of the electric tattoo guns had diminished.

"It looks like your show is ending," I said.

Erzulie smiled. "We're just getting started. Today was our first day, and we are running through the whole weekend."

Chelsea chimed in, "Now we're all going to the pool party."

Erzulie nodded her head knowingly and said, "I believe Doctor Poe needs to get home, but Detective Martin can certainly stay for our *fête*."

I had hoped to get more information and felt that I was leaving disappointed. Despite our failure, Frank, who agreed to stay for the pool party, didn't seem disappointed at all.

13
"Sunshine Superman" - Donovan

Dinner at the Poe household is one of the many wonders of my life. Christina is an excellent cook and works hard to make healthy and delicious food for our family, but she also strives to not be repetitive. Tonight, she had prepared salmon with a guava glaze, green beans, and broccoli.

Lizard had not eaten a vegetable in the past year, and the dinner conversation always turned to trying to convince him that he needed to eat more than just meat.

"I don't like broccoli," he said with a pout.

"I made this especially for you, Lizard, and I want you to eat it," Christina implored, and then she turned to me for support. "Daddy?"

"Lizard, you have to at least try it," I ruled emphatically.

Danielle smiled and finished the last bit of vegetables on her plate. "Mommy, can I have more broccoli please? It's so good."

Christina smiled and scooped more broccoli onto her plate.

"See Lizard, your sister likes the broccoli," Christina cajoled.

"She likes dresses, too, but I'm not going to wear one of those," he responded.

"You don't get to speak to your mother in that tone of voice, young man," I scolded reminding myself of my own father when I was Lizard's age. "Now let's see you take a taste."

Lizard made a face and carefully shoveled a tiny spoonful of broccoli into his mouth.

Hoping to change the subject Christina asked, "How was the tattoo convention?"

"Pretty interesting," I admitted, "but we didn't get the information we were looking for."

"When I grow up I want to get a tattoo!" Lizard piped in through his mouthful of broccoli.

"No, you don't! Only when you start eating your vegetables on your own will we consider tattoos." That was all Christina said to that.

14
"It's a Sunshine Day" -The Brady Bunch

I don't like to wake up early on Saturday mornings, but I had asked Frank to meet me that morning at Lincoln Road Mall so we could go to the beach there. Erzulie had called me during the night and had recognized the tattoo. She remembered that there was a woman who frequented this popular beach every Saturday morning and wondered if it was our victim. I figured Frank and I could find some people who had known Lourdes, and we could hopefully get some new information from them.

I had kidded Frank about the night before, and asked him how everything had worked out at the pool party. Frank groaned and told me it had been fantastic but that he had had too many drinks. He said it got pretty wild in the pool, but he finally left only after promising Erzulie that he would come to her for a free tattoo. Frank was initially hesitant to let me be involved in canvassing the beach with him as this was police business, but a sense of nostalgia won him over.

"When was the last time we were checking out the girls on the beach together?" he said while he laughed.

It had been a long time. I remembered a time when Frank and I were younger when we would spend entire days at the beach. While I was able to tan, Frank's skin would blister, and he was a painful shade of pink most summers. These were different times, and we knew better than to cook in the sun now. When I met Frank in front of Books & Books, he looked no worse for wear from the night before except for his swollen eyelids which he tried to keep covered with his sunglasses. He gave me a look like I was crazy.

"What the hell are you wearing?" he asked.

I looked down at my long-sleeved sun protective shirt, lifted my broad-brimmed hat back, and smiled.

"SPF 60 and you?"

He laughed. "Shit, Harry, you look like a flasher or some other kind of weirdo!"

"Frank, I'm a dermatologist, and if I can't be a role model for good sun protection, how can I expect my patients to follow my advice?"

We walked briskly east toward the beach. Frank handed me a picture of Lourdes Rivera to help me find people who might recognize her.

"If you find even the slightest lead, you need to call me over immediately, and don't start any questioning without me."

"No problem, Frank."

At the east end of Lincoln Road, we crossed Washington Avenue, then the tourist-filled Collins Avenue, and squeezed our way between the Ritz-Carlton and the Loews Hotel. It was only 8:00 a.m., but the beach was already packed.

Where do all these people come from?

I liked to give my older patients credit because they grew up in a time when they were told that sun exposure and sun tanning were healthy. These days I couldn't open a newspaper or magazine without reading about skin cancer. Even women's magazines like *Vogue* and the dreaded *Cosmopolitan* consistently had articles about preventing premature aging of the skin by using protection from the damaging rays of the sun. Despite these widely reported facts, people continued to line up to lie out at the beach. In fact, the only thing that had changed since I was a kid was that the bathing suits had gotten smaller.

"All these people laying out here look like seals on a shoreline," Frank noted.

"Hey Frank, do you know what Tiger Woods and baby seals have in common?"

Frank gave me a look, and I knew he was getting tired of all the Tiger Woods jokes. Frank had been a big fan and, as an avid golfer, he had put Mr. Woods on such a pedestal. It was unlikely that a human being could attain such perfection. He humored me.

"No, I don't."

"They both get clubbed by Scandinavians." The rumor was that Tiger's Swedish wife had taken a golf club to him upon learning of his infidelities.

"Not bad. Now you go north, and I'll go south. If you get a bite, text me. If we come up empty-handed, you're buying lunch."

Frank walked off, and I headed behind the Ritz-Carlton. I noticed a group of young women pointing at me and laughing at my get-up. I walked directly over to them, and they got immediately nervous. I reached into my pocket, brought out some samples of sunscreen, and offered them to the bathing beauties. They took them.

"You like my outfit?" I offered.

There was only one male in their group, and he piped up protectively, "What's the point of coming to the beach like that?"

"I don't want to get damaged by the sun," I answered him, staying friendly.

"That's my point," the young man continued. "Why come to the beach at all if you don't want the sun?"

He had a great point. This is the problem that the Florida tourism industry has to wrestle with. They promote a behavior and lifestyle which brings millions of tourists to soak up the Florida sun, and this helps business. But too much of a "good" thing can cause cancer.

"I'm actually looking for someone, and I'm hoping you can help me."

I produced the photo that Frank had given me and passed it to the young man.

"She's hot! No wonder you're looking for her, old man," he said as the girls giggled. He showed the picture to the girls, and I noticed one of the girls' jaw drop slightly.

I squatted in the sand in front of her. She wore a lime green bikini, and her skin was a dark brown. Her green eyes flew open when I asked her, "Do you recognize her?"

"No, I'm sorry," she said.

I moved my butt into the sand and made myself comfortable. I pulled out my new iPhone.

"Do any of you know how to text message on an iPhone?" I looked around at the ladies.

One of the girls grabbed my phone.

"I'll show you."

With a few finger motions on the touch pad, she was ready.

"Who are you trying to text?"

"It should be in my contact list under Frank."

"Okay." She handed the phone back to me, and I typed <u>Come quick</u>!

I looked at the girls and told them the only thing I knew which would keep them from leaving.

"I'm a dermatologist, and I hope you guys will use the sunscreen I gave you."

The girl in the lime green bikini still appeared quite nervous, but her friends began to ask the inevitable questions.

"What kind of make-up do you recommend?"

"Do you think I need liposuction?"

"Does this mole look funny?"

"Do you do Botox?"

The young man of the group just looked on in wonder. I kept the conversation going until Frank showed up.

"Hey guys, I'd like you to meet my friend Frank Martin. He's a detective with the Miami Police."

Immediately lime green picked up her stuff and ran. As Frank chased her, I noticed the tattoo on the small of her back -- a white horse.

15
"Sunshine Highway"- Dropkick Murphys

Frank caught up to "Little Miss Suntan" in less than twenty yards. I walked over to them as I saw him flashing his badge.

"Ma'am, I'd like to see your identification."

"I didn't do anything wrong," she replied with a whine.

"Upon introduction of me as an officer of the law, you ran. In my line of work this is commonly considered suspicious behavior. Now show me your driver's license, or we'll go downtown to sort this out."

The girl reached into her bag and pulled out a leather wallet. She opened it to her driver's license and handed it to Frank.

"Miss Georgia Felix of 15801 Prestwick Place Miami Lakes." He had pulled out a notepad and wrote this info down.

"Why were you running from us, Georgia?"

"I told you I've done nothing wrong."

"You're not in any trouble here. We are investigating a murder."

"A murder?"

"Yes."

At that moment, Georgia Felix swooned and collapsed on the sand. I reached forward and adjusted her position so she was flat on her back. I grabbed her towel and handed it to Frank.

"Go get this towel wet. Hurry!"

Frank raced over to the showers.

Georgia Felix lay on her back, her face coated with a fine sheen of perspiration. Her green eyes fluttered, and she began to awaken.

"What's going on?"

"Ms. Felix, you fainted."

She tried to sit up, and I gently grabbed her shoulder to prevent it.

"Try to relax. Detective Martin will be back with a cold towel in just a moment."

Frank showed up on cue, and I draped the towel across her neck.

"Does that feel better?"

"Yes."

"Okay, just relax."

"I'm sorry, I don't know what came over me."

"It's hot," I offered, knowing that she was suffering from some form of anxiety attack.

"That must be it," she agreed.

"Sometimes when you're hungry it's easier to faint, too."

"Yes, I guess I'm hungry, too."

"Well, why don't we take you to lunch? It's the least we could do." I looked at Frank. "Detective Frank is paying."

"I guess that would be okay," she agreed.

"Do you think you're ready to sit up?"

"Yes."

Frank grabbed one hand and I grabbed the other and, with a quick pull, Ms. Georgia Felix was back on her feet.

"Shall we go to the Meat Market?" I offered.

The Meat Market was a relatively new addition to Lincoln Road Mall, and it boasted high end atmosphere with first class food.

***

Her name was Georgia Felix, and apparently she had an appetite that belied her athletic figure. Frank whistled when she finished a sixteen ounce prime rib and asked for dessert.

"I guess you were hungry?" he offered, shooting me a look like the girl was breaking his bank.

"I still am," she said with a smile. " I work out every day, and I teach salsa dancing at night. It's the only way I could stay in shape."

"She's keeping a healthy figure, wouldn't you say, Doc? In your expert opinion, of course?" Frank smiled.

"Georgia, I'm more interested in your tattoo. Can you tell me and Detective Martin about it?"

I had been waiting for Frank to start the questioning and, with the niceties out of the way, I thought it was time to break the ice. Frank interrupted before she could answer.

"You know I need to take you down to the station to make a statement so you don't have to answer our questions now. You'll probably have to repeat yourself."

"That's all right. I'll tell you whatever you need to know."

Frank continued.

"Well, first off, why did you run from us back at the beach?"

She looked coolly at the detective, then glanced over at me.

"After the doctor showed me the picture of the woman with the tattoo, I got really nervous. She has a tattoo just like mine."

"Not exactly," I pointed out.

Frank and Georgia both turned to look at me.

I continued, "Georgia, your horse is running to the left while the victim's horse was running to the right. Also does your tattoo fluoresce?"

"What do you mean?"

"Does it glow in the dark?" Frank asked.

"Only if I'm under a black light."

"Tell us about your tattoo, Georgia," I offered.

"There's not much to tell. I love horses," she answered matter-of-factly with a wistful smile.

"Where did you get it done?" I asked.

"Right here on South Beach." She made an expansive practiced display of her arm which showed off her chest nicely as if she was pointing at a particular shop.

"I might know the artist. Which shop did you go to?" I pressed.

"You know that one that was on TV ..." she equivocated.

"Tattoos by Lou?" I offered.

"Yes, that's the one."

I smiled.

"Miami Ink was the television show. I remember Kat Von D."

"Oh, yeah, that must have been it." She recovered but lied poorly.

Frank piped in, "Ms. Felix, have you ever been to Venezuela?"

16
"Don't Let the Sun Go Down on Me" - Elton John

Sister San Juana was visibly shaken. She looked up at me as she cleaned up the bloody towels and put the surgical instruments into the sink.

"El doctor, you should stay away from that man. He's nothing but trouble."

"I'm sure he's harmless, Sister," I said optimistically.

"He's much feared in our community, and I'm terribly worried about what he'll do next."

"Why is he so feared? He's but one man and not a very big man at that."

"El doctor, I'm sorry you have patients waiting to see you, but I'll answer all of your questions after dinner."

At dinner that night the nuns prayed with an intensity like I hadn't seen before. Christina was aware of their nervousness, and I told her about my run-in with Emeliano.

"Do we need to worry?" she asked.

"I don't think so, but Sister San Juana wants to talk after dinner."

The Sisters ate politely and offered refills on the piping hot coffee that we had come to love. I declined because I didn't want to be up all night. When everyone was finished eating, Sister San Juana motioned for Christina and me to follow her into the little chapel.

The chapel was only a small one-roomed building in the courtyard of the clinic compound. It had a small crucifix on the wall opposite the entrance. There were two wooden benches with kneeling pads before them and a rail that separated the makeshift pews from the altar.

Sister San Juana genuflected, crossed herself, and sat in one of the pews. Christina and I followed suit and sat next to her.

Sister San Juana seemed to ponder what she was going to do next. After a full minute of contemplative silence she whispered, "There's something going on in this country. Something dangerous."

She crossed herself again and continued, "Let the Father forgive me for speaking badly of others, but these men you dealt with today are part of the movement."

She whispered those two words, "the movement", with such fear that I felt Christina shudder.

"The movement?" I whispered.

"Shhhh!" She scolded me.

"They have people everywhere, and they report on you, and if they don't like what you're doing, they make trouble for you. I'm afraid they'll make trouble for you, el doctor."

"Are they communists?" Christina whispered.

"They say they're not but they lie. They have little tolerance for people of faith, and they're becoming more and more powerful. Many good people have disappeared. I think the only reason they leave us alone is because everyone needs the clinic."

At that moment one of the many young girls who worked at the clinic and were called collectively the "*muchachas*" interrupted us.

"Excuse me, Mother San Juana. I'm so sorry to interrupt you and el doctor. But something has happened to Ursus -- He's dying!"

Sister San Juana stood quickly, crossed herself, and grabbed me by the arm. "It's starting."

As we bolted out of the chapel, we heard several of the "*muchachas*" crying and wailing and we made our way to them at the front of the compound. As I approached the *muchachas* murmured "el doctor" reverentially and the Sisters made room to let me get a closer look at the animal.

Ursus was on his side, and he was still breathing, but with difficulty. He made a soft whimpering noise that sounded like a child's plastic squeeze toy. He was bleeding from his mouth and nose, and he had defecated a bloody stool. Blood was smeared all over his hind quarters. He even had blood pouring from his eyes.

"What happened?" I asked.

"*Chavistas*," said Sister Francesca. She hissed that word between clenched teeth, and the other sisters gave her reproachful looks.

Sister San Juana looked to Sister Francesca and spoke to me and Christina.

"They do this all the time. First, they put a little poison into some *carne* and wrap it in a tortilla, then they throw it over the wall to poison the guard dogs. Then, when the dog is dead, they'll force their way in and steal whatever they want."

I asked Sister San Juana if she had any Vitamin K. She looked at me funny.

I tried it in better Spanish, "*Vitamina Ka*?"

"Yes," she answered.

"Bring it quickly with a syringe."

She returned immediately with the syringe and a bottle of vitamin K.

I drew up the syringe and injected it into the hip of the dog. He was doing so badly he didn't even react to the injection.

"Will that help, el doctor?" Sister Francesca asked with hope in her eyes.

"With God's help," I said.

At that the nuns and the *muchachas* got on their knees and began praying for their dog. Christina joined the prayer group, and I marched over to the surgery room. I needed to find a weapon if we were going to be attacked.

I looked through all the equipment we had and found a medieval looking bone saw which looked cool, but was next to worthless as a weapon.

I went into the infirmary and looked in on the patients. As I checked on Leal, the poor comatose boy, I heard a voice from under his bed call out to me, "El doctor."

I crouched down and saw that the boys' parents were huddled under the bed. The father adjusted his belt and handed me his machete with a big smile. I took the weapon and shook his hand.

"*Muchas gracias, Señor*." I smiled back.

I stood and stepped into the courtyard, grabbed a chair from the dining room, and sat it down next to the ladies still praying over the dog. After thirty minutes, Ursus virtually rose from the dead. He stood and shook his head, sending bloody spit in all directions. Sister Francesca smiled through her tears and stroked his head, whispering, "*Pobrecito*." He let out a howl to let everyone know that he was still large and in charge.

Christina smiled at me and kissed me on the cheek.

"What are we going to do?" she asked.

"Ask the Sisters to put the coffee on. It's gonna be a long night."

17
"Walkin' on Sunshine" - Katrina & the Waves

Georgia Felix looked surprised.

"Venezuela? Why do you ask?"

"Your tattoo is a horse design from the Venezuelan coat of arms."

She looked from me to Frank. "What do you mean?"

I asked her to stand and show us her tattoo, which she did. The lunch patrons in the restaurant shot reproachful looks at Frank and me like we were dirty old men. Maybe we were, but this was important. I pointed at the horse and looked at Frank.

"As I mentioned before, Georgia's horse is running to the left, and notice its head is not looking backwards. The inks used appear similar to our victim's, but this is certainly a different design."

Frank took a picture with his cell phone, and I asked Georgia to sit back down.

"When Hugo Chavez came to power in Venezuela, he set to work reshaping the society and government." I told Frank, "As part of his changes, he removed the original horse from the country's national seal or coat of arms and replaced it with a stallion to represent his own ideology. One that was running decidedly to the left."

I looked at Georgia and calmly asked for her help.

"Can you tell us the truth about your tattoo now? It may help us stop a killer."

Georgia looked down, and her shoulders heaved, then she raised her face and slowly opened her eyes. "I don't see what's in this for me." she started, then thinking better of herself, continued. "I'll tell you what I can. I never wanted the tattoo, but it was part of the deal."

Frank nodded and put his hand on top of hers on the table between us. "Why don't you start at the beginning?"

"You guys seem like gentlemen, and it's hard for me to talk about this because I don't want to get anyone in trouble."

"Just tell us the truth, and I'm sure you'll feel the burden lifted," Frank empathized.

"Well, last year I was still living in New Jersey. I was feeling pretty bad about myself. I had just gone through a painful break-up, and I was really unhappy. I thought I'd feel better about myself if I had some cosmetic surgery. I looked around, but everywhere I went was way outside my financial possibilities. On top of that, the State of New Jersey charges a tax for cosmetic surgery which makes it even more expensive. I got even more depressed until a friend told me to go to this website about a doctor in Venezuela who did all these great things and was much, much cheaper."

"Can you tell me the doctor's name?" Frank asked.

"Doctor Roto. He's a great guy. I contacted his office via email, and they helped make all the arrangements for my trip there. As part of the package, I got to enjoy a week of recovery on Margarita Island at a Caribbean resort. This whole experience including the surgery, recovery, and travel, would cost about a third of what it would cost here."

"What did you have done?" I asked.

Georgia adjusted her posture to accentuate her chest. "Well, I had my breasts done, laser hair removal, Botox and fillers, and I had some lipo-sculpting."

I ran these procedures in my mind and expected the cost in Miami for this menu of surgery would run close to $25,000 minimum.

"How much did it cost?"

"Well, that's the thing ... when I flew to Caracas, I was met by one of Doctor Roto's nurses who accompanied me to Margarita Island. On the way, we had a great time together, and she told me about the surgery and what I could expect. Her name was Ana, and she was so much fun. She told me that Dr. Roto offered an opportunity for patients if they wanted a discount on his services. This sounded interesting, so I listened."

"She told me that if I was willing to work for the Venezuelan consulate in Miami as a hostess they would provide the services to me for free. I couldn't understand why they would want me to be a hostess for their country, but Ana told me that the new government valued the beauty of the female body and that they wanted to promote Venezuela as *the* destination for plastic surgery and beauty treatments."

"Afterward we arrived on Margarita Island, I met Dr. Roto, and he was so nice and fatherly that I really ... I don't know how to say it ... but I felt comfortable there. It was so beautiful, and everyone was so nice that I agreed to become a hostess."

"The staff was really supportive and when I woke up from sedation, I needed their help. I mean, I've never been in so much pain, but they helped me through it and my recovery ended up taking about two weeks, but that was all covered in our agreement.

"I remember when they helped remove my compression garments and I got the first look at my new body. I was so happy with my breasts and, when I turned to look at my new butt in the mirror, I was shocked."

She fell silent for a moment, and Frank gripped her hand on the table. A small tear welled up in the corner of her right eye. She patted Frank's hand.

"The horse tattoo was there. I asked them what happened, and when no one could answer me, I started to freak out. Finally, Ana came in and got me to relax. She told me that all the hostesses have the white horse tattoo, and that it's something to be proud of. I was now part of the stable. She also invited me to stay another week at their expense and, as I was feeling better, I could really enjoy myself more."

"Did you enjoy yourself?" I asked.

"Oh yes. We went to the beach and to some awesome parties and met so many wonderful people. But all good things come to an end, and I came back to the USA and started my new job in Miami with my beautiful new body and my new tattoo."

"Have you been working at the consulate?" Frank asked.

"Of course. It's a lot of fun and, in this economy, the pay is good."

"Have you met any other hostesses?" Frank asked.

"Oh yes, there are quite a few of us. We work shifts at the Venezuelan welcome station at the consulate and at special events."

Frank smiled. "Are there any special events coming up?"

18

"Sunshine On My Shoulders" -John Denver

When I got back home, Christina was furious. I had forgotten that the Broders were having a cookout, and I was expected to work the barbecue.

"I'm sorry," I told her. I had learned early that those two words were the most important thing a man could say to his wife. Christina gave me an exasperated look, then melted quickly.

"What were you doing?"

"I told you that Frank and I had a lead on that murder case."

"And it just so happens that involves you and him down at the beach leering at all the bikini girls."

I gave her a kiss on the cheek.

"I wouldn't call it leering exactly. Ogling, maybe."

I had let Christina in on a private ongoing conversation that Frank and I have about the subtle difference between leering and ogling. Ogling is what a man does when he looks at a fine specimen of womanhood with appreciation. Leering, however, is when a man looks approvingly at a woman, but wears his imagination all over his face. It's a fine line, but I contend that ogling is harmless.

"The sights were that good, huh?" she teased me with a slap on the back.

"You don't know the half of it, Christina. We met a girl who had a tattoo just like the victim's."

"Harry, don't you think you're getting too involved in this case?"

I could sense the worry in her voice and tried to reassure her. "Don't worry, sweetie. I'm sure Frank appreciates my help."

"I just don't like you getting involved in murder. I mean, there are dangerous people out there."

"I know," I told her, but I didn't.

Within an hour, the cookout was in full swing. Hannah and Christina had made a wonderful array of salads and delicious appetizers. Broder and I hunched over the barbecue grilling ribs and chicken.

Broder was lecturing me about the fine points of barbecuing chicken. "Boy Scout Chicken is what it's called. Burnt on the outside and raw on the inside. You have to keep the chicken from cooking too quickly so that it has time to cook evenly through and through."

"This isn't my first time grilling, counselor," I chastised him for being so critical of my apparent well-trained barbecue skills.

"I gave one of your colleagues a grilling this week," he said sheepishly, trying to get me to bite into his sandwich of gossip.

"Spare me your weak attempt to get me to socialize with you on your low-down lawyer level."

Broder knew I despised what he did for a living, but he was a real sport about letting me bust his hump about it.

"I know you love me, Doc. There's no reason to get your panties in a bunch. This is just business."

I sighed.

"I know I can't get you to think like a normal human being, but the majority of your cases feature a doctor who's trying his best to help someone not hurt someone."

"I agree with you, but accidents happen, and someone has to take responsibility."

"That's just it. You're punishing those who take the responsibility of helping, and it makes it harder for anyone to do anything extraordinary. They become too frightened of being sued."

"I hear this story over and over again, and its just a rationalization. Doctors are paid to help people and, when things go right, they get paid, but when things go wrong they should expect to pay for it."

"But they're paying you."

"Why shouldn't they? My services are valuable. I help my clients get the most out of insurance companies that they can."

"And if you destroy a few reputations along the way or scare a settlement out of the insurance company even when your case isn't strong enough to go to a trial? Then that's okay?"

"I always think you're blaming me personally, but I didn't set up this adversarial system, and I can understand your aggravation. I do my best to navigate my clients to a monetary reward."

"You take your third right or wrong." I flipped the ribs with the tongs accidentally putting my face into the smoke, then brushed the tears from my eyes with the back of my hand.

"You always take this way too personally. It's business. It's what I do, and I'm damn good at it. You don't expect me to do it for free?"

I wiped the last of the smoky tears from my eyes and turned to meet Broder's gaze.

"I provide services for patients every day, and I get paid for them. My patients expect my very best. But if they can't afford to pay me, I see them for free, and I still do my best for them."

Broder stumbled in his conversation. "I ... uh ... I think that's admirable, Harry, and I don't want you to think I haven't done pro bono work myself, but I think it's great that you help out so many poor people."

I grabbed a rib with the tongs and placed it on a paper plate and handed it to him to try.

"It's hot," I warned him.

Broder grabbed the rib and bit into it gingerly. His face took on a studious countenance while he chewed like he was an expert tasting a fine wine. His smile lit up his wide face.

"It's good, Doc."

I smiled.

"You know, if more doctors saw people for free, I think it would certainly help your profession's image."

This advice about doctors' public image, I remind you, is coming from a bonafide ambulance chasing personal injury attorney.

"We all do it," I humbly corrected him.

"Well, they ought to make a law that forced doctors to do what you do."

I set down my tongs and started all over again with my best friend, Broder. "I know I can't get you to think like a normal human being, but if you make that a law, then it would no longer be charity work that we do. I don't think anyone would feel good about doing it anymore. Would the law be enforced at gunpoint or with monetary fines and taxation? Would the newly entitled poor demand more and more from those who before were giving of themselves freely? Would a whole new government agency be put in charge of coordinating this charity work? The bottom line is that forced charity isn't charity at all."

Broder looked down and saw Little Pinch looking up at his rib bone with greed in her eyes.

"Looks like I can at least offer a little charity to your dog."

He tossed the bone on the ground before her, and Little Pinch didn't move.

Broder patted her huge head.

"Go on, girl, you can have that delicious rib bone."

Still, she didn't move.

Then, only her eyes moved. They turned toward me longingly, then I gave her the signal. I brought my right index finger and middle finger together like a scissors snap, and Little Pinch pounced on that bone with serious gusto.

Broder laughed and patted her big head again. "Good dog."

We turned to watch the beautiful tropical sunset that South Florida is known for and, in the gloaming, we could hear the laughter of our children playing.

19
"We'll Sing in the Sunshine" - Dolly Parton

Day by day, everybody looks forward to the weekend. How we spend our time on these special days speaks volumes about our priorities and interests. My wife Christina devotes her Sundays to church and horses.

She fell in love with horses late in life. Most little girls grow up asking their daddies for a pony and dreaming of having a horse of their very own. Christina was too practical for that fantasy even as a little girl.

That all changed when Hannah invited her to their stable in Wellington, which is high-end horse country west of Palm Beach. There she learned first-hand the thrills of dressage, English and Western styles, and barrel racing. Hannah loved the company, and soon she and Christina were taking riding lessons with the master horseman of South Florida, Cole Julius. Julius was a grizzled old cowboy who sold his services as a "horse whisperer" and was renowned as a serious mentor.

He promised Christina and Hannah that they would be able to "cut cattle" when he was finished with them. This was a wonderful term for an aggressive method of herding cattle on horseback. It's a high adrenaline activity and requires extreme skills from the rider and a horse of above average intellect. There was just one problem. Christina needed her own horse.

Before I could blink, we were the proud owners of a fine young mare named Amber, and Christina was devoted to her. A giant red roan quarter horse, Amber was beautiful to look at, but a holy terror if you were a cow.

This particular Sunday, the kids and I accompanied Christina to the stables, and we watched appreciatively as she tended to her horse's lame hoof. She applied the foul-smelling antibiotic with a delicate firmness, and Amber seemed content to let her fuss at her while she cleaned and wrapped the wound. Mr. Julius had reassured us that the horse's lameness would pass, and Amber would be back to herself within the week.

The kids and I looked around at the other horses in the large boarding stables, and I was struck by all the women involved in caring for these huge animals. Sure, there were cowboys like Cole Julius, but the equestrian scene by and large was dominated by women. Some treated their horses like their babies, and some treated them like their lovers, so you would often hear the owners cooing over their "baby" or "sweetie" or even bragging about their "stud."

Cole confided in me during a private moment that "horse people" were all crazy. Crazy or not, I was glad that it made Christina happy. A wise man once said, "Happy wife. Happy life." I believed him.

I thought about my life and counted the many blessings I had received, like healthy children and a loving wife. I was reminded again of poor Lourdes Rivera and all that she had lost.

20
"Give Me Some Sunshine" - from the Bollywood film *The Three Idiots*

To go on record, Frank didn't want me to do it. Christina didn't want me to do it. But, to be perfectly honest, I felt a thrill as I called the Miami consulate office of Venezuela.

Georgia had told us about an event which was tailor-made for my help with the investigation. The Venezuelan consulate was hosting a doctors-only reception to encourage referrals to their popular plastic surgery services.

The consulate maintained an office on the upscale Brickell Avenue in a building that shared space with the consulates of Bolivia and Ecuador. If Cuba had been allowed to have an embassy in our country, I'm sure they would have their consulate in the same building.

The phone rang three times, and a recorded voice told me in Spanish that I had reached the office of the consulate of The Bolivarian Republic of Venezuela. If I wanted to speak in English I was to press the number nine.

I pressed it, and another recording welcomed me again, but in English. I was told the hours of operation from 9:00 a.m. to 1:00 p.m. and that the doors close at 12:00 p.m. If I wanted to speak to an operator, I was instructed to dial zero.

I did.

"Hello, welcome to the consulate of the Bolivarian Republic of Venezuela. How may I direct your call?" Hers was a beautiful voice that spoke perfect English with the right amount of Spanish accent that made her sound sexy and business-like at the same time.

"Hi, my name is Doctor Harold Poe, and I'm interested in attending your plastic surgery reception."

"Thank you, Doctor Poe. I'm connecting you with Manuel Rojas our special events coordinator."

I held the line for a minute and classical music played. A heavily accented male voice interrupted the musical interlude.

"Ah, Doctor Poe, your reputation as a great dermatologist precedes you. My name is Manuel."

I'm sure that he must have looked me up in the yellow pages while I was waiting and was now putting on the charm.

"I don't know if this reception would be best for you as I see you do offer cosmetic procedures in your office."

"I only do Botox and fillers," I reassured him. "Most of my practice is treating skin cancer."

"I see. Well, we're hoping to make local doctors aware of the expertise of our plastic surgeons and hopefully influence your referrals."

I played a little hard to get.

"Will I be able to find out about pricing? In this economy, my patients are looking for deals."

"Why, of course, Doctor Poe. I assure you that you will find our techniques and results exemplary, and your patients will appreciate the bargain."

He told me the location for the reception at a mansion on Star Island. Dress was business casual, and they would be serving hors d'oeuvres and dinner.

"Should I bring a date, Manuel?"

"Oh no, Doctor, this reception is for medical professionals only and, to tell you the truth ...

how you say? You don't want to bring a sandwich to a buffet."

I scribbled the address down, thanked Manuel, and hung up. I turned to look at Frank. He read the expression on my face.

"What's so funny?" he asked.

"Looks like I'm going to a Venezuelan fiesta!"

21
"Good Day Sunshine" - The Beatles

The night Ursus was poisoned passed without incident, and things seemed to get back to normal at the clinic when Doctor Marcos finally returned two days later. Sister San Juana told him about all the patients we treated, which medicines were used, and what was left in the pharmacy. When Dr. Marcos was confident that he was up to date on all the patients and the state of affairs of the clinic, she told him about our run-in with Emeliano and Javíer and the poisoning of the dog.

Dr. Marcos asked her to bring two cups of coffee and invited me to follow him into his office. He asked me to be seated and eased himself into the old chair behind his desk.

"Harry, you've done great work, and I'll surely send a nice letter of thanks and recommendation to your medical school. As only a fourth year student, you handle yourself well enough that I'm confident that you'll be a great doctor. I say these things because I want you to know how appreciative we all are for what you were able to do for the last two weeks, but also because I must ask you to leave."

"Leave?" I was dumbfounded. "I still have two more weeks left of my rotation with you."

"I know." He spread his hands wide. "If there was any other way ... I could surely use your help around here but I'm afraid it's a matter of safety."

"Are you talking about Emeliano?"

"Shhh!" he hissed. "Lower your voice, please. The men you insulted are bad men. They'll come back and they'll seek their revenge upon you.. or worse. The Sisters, the clinic, your wife are all in danger."

"Revenge?" I whispered. "I didn't do anything to that man except help his friend."

"San Juana says that you refused to pay him and that you laughed at him."

"This is ridiculous. Do you have to pay him to help people?"

Doctor Marcos looked down. "I pay them something every month. I try to barter services with them instead, but their demands keep increasing. They threaten the people, and their spies are everywhere."

"Who are they? Can you call the police?"

Doctor Marcos didn't have to explain much to me, because I knew my history.

"They're *communistas*."

No amount of pleading or rationalizing on my part could satisfy Doctor Marcos. He made arrangements with Sister San Juana that we were to leave in the morning.

I did my best to reassure Christina, but she became uncomfortably nervous. The Sisters told us that they would prepare a special dinner for us that night, and they wouldn't allow Christina to help in the preparation.

Evening prayer in the clinic's little chapel took on a special urgency, and the *muchachas* couldn't hide their frequent furtive looks of concern. Sister San Juana rapped one of the girls on her interlaced fingers and told her to look to the altar.

We went into the dining room and were surprised by the delicious aromas of a pork roast. I knew that this was a particularly prized meal for the Sisters and Doctor Marcos. Before we started eating, Doctor Marcos said grace and included in the blessing a request to, "please grant your protection to our American friends and keep them safe." The Sisters appeared a little nervous that the prayer may have been too loud, but smiled and offered the food to Christina first.

We dug into the succulent pork and the yucca. The garlic and chiles seasoned the meat to perfection. We washed this down with piping mugs of fresh coffee. Doctor Marcos entertained us with stories of when he first opened the clinic. We were surprised to find out that Sister San Juana had been dropped off at the clinic as an infant with the expectation of death.

Doctor Marcos treated her septicemia with broad spectrum antibiotics, and after two months she was thriving again. When her parents returned, they told Doctor Marcos that they couldn't care for her and that she was his now since he had saved her. He raised her as his own with the help of the Sisters, and she ultimately left to take Holy Orders to become a nun and eventually returned to the clinic to help as soon as she could.

I wondered how I had missed the obvious adoration they had for each other and remained surprised by my lack of observational skills.

The plan was made that San Juana would drive us to Father Lorenzo's church, then we would make our way back to Canaima and eventually Caracas and home.

It was at that moment that a loud crashing noise came from the front of the clinic compound.

22
"Ain't No Sunshine" - Bill Withers

Star Island is one of those premiere locations in the world where only the ultra-rich elite can afford to live. It sits in the middle of Biscayne Bay between Miami Beach and Miami and is the ultimate gated community. In Dade County, there's a special tax on waterfront homes so beside the cost of the home, the yearly property taxes on these mansions would be enough to buy a normal house.

There's a cottage industry of tourist boats which will take you around Biscayne Bay, and they'll point out the homes of the rich and famous like Madonna and Sylvester Stallone. I went on one of these tours, and I remember them pointing out a particularly opulent mansion and the tour guide saying that the only person who could afford to live at this home had to be a drug dealer. He was right, but it wasn't illegal drug dealers who owned it, but a pharmaceutical tycoon who made his fortune with generic drugs.

My heart skipped a beat as I realized it was this home that I was pulling past, and next door was the Bolivarian Republic of Venezuela's "bargain basement" plastic surgery reception.

When I told Frank about the phone call, he demanded that I come down to the Metro Miami Police Department to talk with his superior, Commander Jimenez. I had met Jimenez before in social gatherings with Frank, but now he was all business.

He thanked me for my willingness to help the department and seemed genuinely worried about my safety.

"Are you going to deputize me?" I had asked.

"What ... do you want a badge?" he asked with smile. "We'd have to put you on the payroll." He laughed.

"I don't think you could afford me," I teased him.

Commander Jimenez continued smiling and said, "Look, Doc, this might seem like fun and games to you, but this is deadly serious. We already have one dead victim, and we don't need another. I only want you to find out if this patient referral program of theirs is legit and if Lourdes Rivera was involved in it."

"I'll do my best," I told him and confidently added, "I'm sure they'll find me charming."

Frank laughed. Jimenez gave him a cold look.

"Remember, Doc, curiosity killed the cat."

Now here I was valet parking my car and walking into a reception that I can only describe as ostentatious. There were buffets of raw oysters and jumbo shrimp. An open bar was stocked with the finest liquors, and over our heads in the grand marble foyer flew a giant Venezuelan flag. On the walls hung a welcome sign in English and Spanish, but the *piece d'resistance* was a giant portrait of one Hugo Chavez whose thick facial features told me that he was extremely well-fed and he might have diabetes. Welcoming me to the reception was a beautiful woman who told me her name was Joelisa, and she brought me to the bar. There she introduced me to another well-fed man wearing a tightly fitting suit and a remarkable gold necklace with an actual gold nugget as a pendant.

"This is Manuel," she offered.

I shook his hand, "I'm Doctor Harold Poe."

Manuel smiled. "Thank you, Joelisa. Doctor Poe, I hope you'll enjoy yourself tonight. As far as I know, you're the only dermatologist here tonight."

I smiled back at him. "I hope I don't get lonely."

"Ha!" laughed Manuel. "That is unlikely tonight, my friend. The presentation will begin in about twenty minutes, Doctor Poe. Until then we want you to mingle and help yourself to the hors d'ouvres and cocktails."

Joelisa smiled. "But save room because we have a full dinner planned during the presentation."

I thanked her, and she turned to walk away. I noted the deep cut of the neckline on the back of her dress which descended to her waistline, and there was the now familiar tattoo of a white horse running to the left.

I turned to the bartender, who gave me a funny look when I asked only for a plain Coke. I sipped my drink and surveyed the crowd.

Among the multitude of typical doctors I spotted a few familiar faces of my colleagues. They were primary care physicians which included family practice, internists, and gynecologists. Being a plastic surgery seminar, I didn't expect to see any pediatricians present, and I didn't.

Doctors tend to run into two stereotypes. There are the exceptional fashion plates who dress impeccably and the bulk of the rest who tend to have three blazers that they rotate and whose shoulders are invariably covered with a fine dusting of dandruff.

Interestingly, I noticed there were no female doctors among the bunch. Women make up the majority of med school graduates, so the fact that there weren't any present appeared suspicious. Not to say there weren't women present. Running back and forth between the groups of professionals were the hostesses who made sure that the doctors were happy and were getting plenty of drinks.

This was the "stable" that Georgia had mentioned.

I moved to the buffet of oysters on the half shell and set up shop. I was working on my second dozen when Doctor Mario Barquin came over to me to say hello. Doctor Barquin is a family doc whom I share patients with and I know as a truly solid physician, so I have no problem referring my patients to him. He's on staff at Jackson Memorial, the VA, Mt. Sinai, and Cedars, and he has a busy private practice as well.

"Well, Doctor Poe, it's nice to see you out and about."

Mario offered his hand for a strong clasp. I smiled at him conspiratorially.

"What do you make of this, Mario?"

"You know me, Harry, if there's a free buffet, I will check it out, but I haven't used any of their services."

"You're unsure about their surgeons?" I asked.

"Oh, I wasn't talking about the doctors; I was talking about these hostesses."

I guess I gave him a dumbfounded stare because he quickly explained. "Look, Harry, I'm a single man, and these girls are attractive. So I'm tempted, believe me, but I tend to get suspicious when things are too easy."

"What do you mean?" I laughed, expecting a dissertation regarding Mario's skills with the opposite sex and his personal measure of his own self-worth, but I was surprised by his perspective.

"I mean, sometimes it's too easy. Like if a woman melts just because you're a doctor, it doesn't seem real. Like maybe she's a shallow gold-digger. It's the same with these hostesses, who try so hard to make you happy, but you know it's just their job. It's not real."

"Mario, many people find romance on the job." I laughed.

At that moment, Joelisa appeared and invited us into the dining area.

"Gentlemen, the appetizers are being served, and the presentation is about to begin."

She walked us to our seats, and sitting on either side of us was a lovely hostess. On my right was Davetta and on my left, Sofía. Mario sat next to Sofía, and on his left was Miss Georgia Felix who gave me a friendly wink, but other than that gave me no sign that we'd met before or had had a marvelous lunch together on Detective Frank Martin's dime.

Davetta told me that she was originally from Venezuela and that she'd been a finalist in the Miss Universe contest. I could certainly believe it because the term statuesque described her perfectly. She had beautiful brown hair with blonde highlights and a fine copper complexion. She wore a white blouse that had poofy shoulders and a bare midriff. The ensemble came together with a lovely long white skirt that featured slits along the sides up to her hips, showing off her golden high heels. When she bent forward I noticed the ubiquitous horse tattooed on the small of her back.

I took her hand in mine and surprised myself with a forward line of questioning. "Surely you come by your beauty naturally?"

She looked at Sofía, and they both giggled. Davetta told me that all of the hostesses had received any number of cosmetic procedures and that was why they were there, basically, to show them off.

"Americans are so repressed about plastic surgery," interjected Sofía.

I wondered aloud if she had ever been to Beverly Hills. She, too, was tall like a supermodel, but the most striking feature of hers was a platinum blonde head of hair. She had ice blue eyes and the milky pale skin that would make any Scandinavian proud.

"In Venezuela, we consider plastic surgery a necessity."

I asked them about the horse tattoos, and they proudly showed me theirs. They told me that being part of Doctor Roto's stable has been not only financially lucrative, but had opened up a lot of opportunities for them in public relations and in local fashion.

I asked if they knew all the hostesses, and Davetta said that she did because she and Joelisa were some of the first women to join "the stable."

"I have a friend named Lourdes Rivera who has a horse tattoo, but I never heard her tell me about the stable."

Davetta looked over to Sofía, and they both shook their heads.

"I don't know of any Lourdes that has ever been one of our hostesses," answered Davetta, and I felt like she was telling me the truth.

Relishing the attention from these two beautiful women, I complimented Sofía on her skin tone and asked which brand of sunscreen she used. This eventually led them to the realization that I was a dermatologist, and the steady streams of questions began all over.

"Do you do Botox?" asked Sofía.

"Do you do liposuction?" asked Davetta.

"Well, I devote most of my practice to the treatment and prevention of skin cancer, but I do a little cosmetic work."

Davetta pulled her skirt away from her left thigh and pointed out a tiny array of interlacing blood vessels.

"Doctor Poe, what can I do about spider veins?"

I gave her my stock answer.

"No one is as critical of you as you are of yourself."

She gave me a blank stare and I added, "I don't think you should worry about that ... it's insignificant."

"To you, maybe, but they drive me crazy."

At that moment, the lights came down, and Joelisa stood in front of us as a movie screen descended behind her.

She carried a wireless microphone and brought it to her lips.

"It's such an honor for us to have so many important members of the medical community here with us tonight. I hope you're enjoying your appetizers, and your entrees will come out during the presentation. Now, without further ado, let me introduce the foremost plastic surgeon of the Bolivarian Republic of Venezuela, Doctor Eduardo Roto."

A well dressed man stepped in front of us and took the microphone from Joelisa.

"Thank you, Joelisa. Let's give her and all our lovely hostesses a big round of applause."

The doctors all clapped, and a few in the back whistled.

"I guess the alcohol's kicking in," I whispered to Sofía, who smiled back at me.

Doctor Roto began his PowerPoint presentation with some beautiful photos of Venezuelan tourist destinations - Caracas, Angel Falls, and Margarita Island. He transitioned from the beautiful locations to showing the many beautiful Venezuelan women who have recently taken home the crown in the Miss Universe beauty pageants.

"Beauty is at the heart of Venezuelan life," he told us. "It's not by accident that our women have been recognized as some of the most beautiful in the world. Recent consecutive wins in the Miss Universe contest have only brought more attention to our country."

He turned to the audience. "Now I'm not saying that I operated on all our winners, but I am pointing out that in Venezuela our quest for physical perfection is second to none."

He motioned to the ladies in the audience.

"All of the beautiful hostesses at our event tonight have received a surgical enhancement of some kind, and they'll be happy to show off our work this evening."

He smiled and continued with the presentation. He outlined the services that he and his colleagues provided, ranging from breast augmentation and liposuction to the "Paris lip" and buttock augmentation. His presentation showed before and after pictures that were of the finest caliber. The photos were taken in the exact same setting, and the lighting seemed identical, so I imagined that they must have a photographic studio at their clinic.

"Surgical enhancement has become common in my country, and our clinic is certainly the top destination for locals and tourists alike looking for our level of expertise. I don't have to tell you that in this economic recession people are looking for better bargains. But I hope my talk tonight has reassured you that if you refer your patients to us they'll not only benefit economically, but also from our first class surgical skills. Thank you."

The room thundered with applause, and the guests began to dig into their entrees with enthusiasm. Filet Mignon and Florida lobster tail made up this version of Surf and Turf. Doctor Roto asked for questions.

From the front row an older Indian physician whose shiny scalp showed through a ring of thinning hair asked, "Where can we find out the prices of your procedures?"

"That's a great question," replied Doctor Roto with an ingratiating smile, "and what is your name doctor?

"Doctor Patel," he answered.

"Ah, thank you, Doctor Patel. Our hostesses will be bringing around pamphlets that outline our à la carte pricing as well as our package deals where a patient can get several procedures done at once."

I raised my hand.

"Do you use silicone as a filler for any of your augmentations?"

"That, too, is a great question because, as you know, injectable silicone is quite controversial. What is your name, doctor?"

"Harry," I answered.

"Doctor Harry brings up an excellent point about injectable silicone. It's controversial because it can migrate into the tissues and cause terrible disfigurements. But in the right hands, medical grade silicone can give excellent results which are far better than other fillers."

He looked out at the audience and called out, "Joelisa, can you come up here?"

Joelisa joined Doctor Roto in front of the audience.

"*Cariño*, can you show the doctors your booty?"

Joelisa smiled and unwrapped her skirt to show off her firm buttocks. She wore only a light green thong.

Doctor Roto slapped her gently on the right buttock, and her large firm moon showed remarkably little jiggle. Joelisa smiled at the appreciative audience. I'm sure I wasn't the only one noticing the white horse tattoo just above her plump derriere.

"This is a butt that puts your famous J Lo to shame and, believe it or not, she has had silicone injections. If any of you would like to feel its natural texture, Joelisa would be only too happy to comply."

Several doctors stepped forward. I looked over at Mario to gauge his reaction and nearly choked on my mouthful of buttered lobster tail. Mario was feeling Georgia's exposed breasts and seemed quite impressed from a strictly professional point of view. I heard the sound of angels harping and fished my new cell phone out of my pocket.

"Hey Sweetie," I answered.

Christina sounded annoyed, "When are you coming home?"

"The party is just getting good," I told her truthfully with a laugh.

"Weekends are meant to be spent with your family," she continued.

"I know, I know, baby. I'll be home soon."

I hung up the phone and noticed Sofía and Davetta staring at me. They looked at each other and laughed.

"What?" I offered.

"Nothing," Davetta said with a devilish grin.

They offered us three different desserts and, when I couldn't make up my mind, they brought me all three, Key Lime Pie, coconut flan, and crème brûlée. The hostesses hardly ate and picked their way around their plates.

The audience was breaking off into small groups, and many of the physicians were palpating the chests and buttocks of the many hostesses. Drinks were filled and refilled. Joelisa gave every doctor a professional services pamphlet, and I figured it was time to go. I noticed Mario had disappeared with Georgia, and I was happy for them both.

I got up from the dinner table to leave and began to say goodbye to the ladies.

Sofía stood with me and said, "You're not leaving so early, Doctor Poe?"

"Yes, I know, but I have to go."

I felt two hands embrace my hips from behind and felt Davetta's warm breath whisper in my ear. "Don't leave yet. We still have something to show you."

Sofía grabbed my hand and led me back to the entranceway. I felt a little foolish with this young girl holding my hand, and I was literally flabbergasted as I followed Sofía into a guest room, and she quickly fell onto the bed.

I laughed and turned to back out, but Davetta blocked my exit and was closing the door behind me.

"I'm sorry, ladies, but I don't really feel comfortable in here alone with you."

I looked over to the bed, and Sofía had removed her clothing except for her thong.

"Does this make you more comfortable?" she asked with a wicked look in her eyes as she crooked her finger enticing me to join her.

I turned back to the door, and Davetta fell into my arms and tried to kiss my neck. I pushed her away.

"Stop it, ladies. This isn't for me."

Davetta smiled. "You say no, but your body is telling me yes!"

I followed her gaze to the front of my pants and was shocked by my own erection. Something wasn't right.

I pushed Davetta aside and opened the door. Standing before me was an ugly man in a finely tailored suit. He barred my way, and I quickly pushed past him before I even recognized him. It was Emeliano.

23
"Sunshine (Go Away Today)" - Jonathan Edwards

The front of the clinic compound had collapsed, and through the rubble of the wall a bulldozer could be seen backing away from the destruction it had caused. Six men with red bandanas around their necks climbed in through the wreckage. They carried with them an assortment of guns.

They pointed their guns at us, and we put our hands up. Doctor Marcos stared hard at the closest man.

"Pedro, how's your mother?" he asked.

Pedro looked into the doctor's face and smiled as if he couldn't possibly be threatening our lives with his gun.

"She's doing well, el doctor. I'll tell her that you asked after her."

"Thank you, Pedro." Doctor Marcos smiled as well.

Pedro walked over to Ursus, who was barking loudly and straining to break out of his chain. He pointed his gun at the angry dog and pulled the trigger. The nuns began to weep in terror as the mighty Ursus hit the ground with a wet slap.

Through the smoke from the rubble came Emeliano and Javier. They, too, wore the red kerchief of the communists around their necks. Emeliano walked past Christina and kissed his fingertips slowly for effect. Then, he stopped and stood before me.

"*El niño* doctor owes me an apology. I'm here to collect it and to collect some taxes."

I felt the pulse in my temples throb as I ground my teeth together instead of saying what I wanted to.

I felt his breath on my face.

"Do you have my money, el doctor? Or should I take it out in trade?"

He leered over at Christina. The nuns stepped in front of her despite the guns pointing at them. Their message was simple but clear - *You'll have to kill us first.*

I could take no more. "Emeliano, be reasonable. I took care of your friend and asked nothing in return."

Emeliano turned his emotionless eyes toward mine, and his voice was filled with anger. "El doctor, you question my reason. A foreigner like you has no understanding of the people. I'm the voice of the people, and you insult us with your very presence. I've never been so disrespected by anyone let alone a capitalist rat like you. For that, I'll make you pay."

Doctor Marcos lowered his hands.

"Don't worry, my friend, we have your taxes right here." He produced an envelope that contained cash. Emeliano grabbed the stack and thumbed through the bills.

"There's six hundred dollars here, el doctor."

"Yes, Emeliano." Doctor Marcos nodded.

Emeliano smiled, but there was no joy in his eyes, only hate. "The tax is only $500."

He handed one hundred dollars back to Doctor Marcos, then turned to his men.

"They've paid in full, and we're reasonable men. We believe in social justice. We shall take our leave."

Then he stepped in front of my face again and hissed into my left ear. "We're not finished, *Americano*!"

He turned toward Doctor Marcos.

"Perhaps you can hire my men with those one hundred dollars you have there."

He motioned toward the rubble.

"It seems you have construction work to be done on your clinic's wall."

He took the rest of the money from Doctor Marcos' still outstretched hand. He smiled at his own cleverness, strolled through the hole in the wall, and his men followed after him.

Doctor Marcos turned to Sister San Juana and whispered, "Get them out of here, now."

24
"That's The Way (I Like It)" - KC & the Sunshine Band

I ran out of the opulent Star Island mansion and throttled the valet for my keys. I demanded to know where he parked my car, and I slipped him a five. I ran to the car's door, turned the key, and hopped in. As I pulled away, I saw Emeliano run out of the house after me. I checked him in the rearview mirror and saw him take out a camera and snap a picture of my car. I reached for my new iPhone, checked the recent calls, and hit Christina's name. My mind said a silent prayer. Please make her pick up. On the third ring, she picked up, and from the drawl of her voice I could tell she'd been sleeping.

"Look, Sweetie, I need you to listen carefully. I want you to take the kids and the dog and go into the safe room and lock yourselves in."

"What's going on?"

"I just ran into Emeliano, our communist friend from Venezuela."

I heard Christina gasp.

"I don't know if we're in any danger, but I'd feel safer knowing you're in the safe room."

The safe room was something we'd made sure to build into our home since we saw first-hand the devastation from Hurricane Andrew. Prior to the hurricane that hit New Orleans, no other storm in recent memory had been so destructive. Christina was sure that if everything collapsed around us that the special fortified room would withstand any assault. Now I was asking her to lock our family inside it. She didn't need much convincing.

After we hung up, I immediately called Frank. He picked up on the first ring.

"How's the party, Doc?"

"Listen Frank, there's some serious stuff going on, and I need you to put a patrol unit in front of my house."

"Are you serious?"

"Absolutely! I recognized someone at the Venezuelan party who has threatened me before."

"Okay, I'll make sure we have a car out front immediately. Are Christina and the kids okay?"

"They will be if you can come through with the protection."

"Should be no problem. Where are you?"

"I'm driving north on Biscayne Boulevard. Can you and Jimenez meet me at the station?"

"I'll be there in fifteen minutes."

I hung up. As I drove past the sights and sounds of Biscayne Boulevard on a Friday night, my mind rushed through the considerable amount of unusual information this case had left me with. I tried to let the puzzle pieces of informational clues roll around in any direction and let my subconscious mind bring them together in some sort of order.

Fluorescent tattoos, Hugo Chavez, and the Bolivarian Republic of communists, scalpel tourism, and the dandruff-covered shoulders of doctors who were old enough to know better. How did Emiliano fit into this puzzle? This was a man I wished never to see again unless it was at his funeral.

What was he doing in Miami, and what was his relationship with the Venezuelan plastic surgeons?

I began to imagine that perhaps the fluorescent tattoos were used to transport secret messages or some type of code that could only be seen under a special light, and perhaps that was why Lourdes's tattoo had been removed.

Why was Lourdes' tattoo different?

Was it older?

Her horse had been running to the right, and this was the older symbol of Venezuela which had been changed by Hugo Chavez to the new horse that ran decidedly to the left. Some people wear their politics on their sleeves, but the hostesses wore theirs on the small of their lovely backs.

But the biggest question that I wanted answered was why I was still sporting a painful erection? Had the Venezuelans actually spiked my food with Viagra or Cialis? Why would they do that, and why were those hostesses so overtly flirtatious? I consider myself a fine enough male specimen, but not the type whom two super-models would wantonly throw themselves at. In public, no less. I hadn't even turned on my charm.

Ah!

I started to see now why Emeliano was outside my door. He took a picture of my car with a camera that was just too handy. Perhaps he was waiting for a moment to snap some compromising pictures of me with the beautiful Davetta and the gorgeous Sofía.

Christina wouldn't like those pictures and neither would any of the married doctors' wives. If they planned to blackmail us, it could just work.

"You must send patients to Dr. Roto's clinic, or we'll show the pictures to your wife. You must give us money, or we'll show the pictures to your wife. You must pay me $500 for helping out the people, the movement, the party, our merry band of thieves."

I thought of Mario. As he was a single man, what could they blackmail him with? A photo with a beautiful woman wouldn't hurt his reputation.

I flicked through the contacts on my new phone and tried to stay in traffic. These cell phones were going to get people killed. I found the listing for Doctor Mario Barquin. I pressed the touch screen and the phone started ringing. Mario picked up on the second ring.

"Hello?"

"Look Mario, I don't have time to talk, but I must warn you! The police are coming to the reception, and there are drugs in the house. You may have been slipped something in your drinks or in your food. You must leave now!"

"*Maricón!*" Mario screamed this expletive into the phone, but believed me immediately. "Okay, okay. I'm leaving." He hung up the phone.

I only hoped that he moved quickly. I pulled into the parking lot of the Metro Miami-Dade Police Department, and Frank was waiting for me.

I stepped out of the car, and Frank burst out, laughing.

"Doc, you know there are laws against smuggling." He motioned to the front of my pants. "What are you packing anyway? A zucchini?"

I gave Frank a look that would melt diamonds.

"Is Jimenez here yet?"

"He's upstairs."

"Do you have a unit guarding my family?"

"Already in place." He held up a hand-held radio. "We'll be the first to hear if there's anything going down."

I felt my muscles in my neck relax just a little. We marched up the stairway to Jimenez's office. He sat behind his desk, spread his hands wide, and smiled.

"You must be happy to see me, Doc."

Frank laughed.

It was my turn to dress down the comedians.

"Listen, you assholes, this is serious."

Their smiles dissolved, and I had their full attention.

"I believe my food as well as the food of every doctor at that reception was laced with some Viagra-like drug. I think the Venezuelans are making sure that the cosmetic surgery business of South Florida is directed to their clinics. I believe these doctors will be photographed in compromising situations and will be blackmailed into compliance.

"No shit, Harry?" Frank was dumbfounded.

"That's not all. A maniac whom I met many years ago in Venezuela was there and was a part of these shenanigans. He's a communist, and he threatened Christina and me at gunpoint over ten years ago, and now he's here. If he were to recognize me, I think he may come after me or my family."

Jimenez was all business now. "Don't worry, Doc. We've two men stationed at your house, and we'll make sure to have a detail there all night."

"Thank you."

"Now sit down and, while it's still all fresh in your mind, I'd like you to fill out a report for us. And I want you to try to remember names and descriptions of people the best that you can."

I called Christina and told her the police were positioned outside the house for protection. I told her I had seen Emeliano at the reception, and I believed he recognized me. She decided to keep the family locked in the safe room until I returned. I said goodbye and turned to give Jimenez my report.

It was a long process; Frank always told me that law enforcement was a great deal of paperwork for very little action. The action kept him going, though, as he was a self-professed adrenaline junkie.

When I finished my account, Jimenez had it notarized, and they asked me to sign it. I did. I looked at my watch.

"It's three a.m. I need to get home."

Frank thanked Jimenez, and we walked out together.

"I'll follow you home," Frank offered.

I nodded.

Even on a Friday night, the streets were quiet at this early hour. My car moved easily through the streets of El Portal, and I soon found myself on the deserted streets of Miami Shores, the lovely suburb of greater Miami that I called home. I pulled onto 92nd Street and saw the police car parked in front of my house. I pulled in, and Frank gave the patrolmen a wave and drove off. I walked over to the car and said hello to the two officers in the car.

"Good evening, gentlemen. Thank you for keeping watch on my home."

"Are you Doctor Poe?" asked the older looking officer.

"Yes, sir."

"I've been trying to get an appointment at your office, and they keep telling me it's a three to four month wait."

"What were you worried about?" I offered.

"I've got a mole that's been bleeding."

"Can you come to my office Monday morning at 8:00 a.m.?"

"Sure"

"I'll see you then." I turned to the house with a parting, "Good night, and thanks again, gentlemen."

I heard the younger officer say to his partner, "Wow, membership sure has its privileges!"

I unlocked the front door, waved to the police officers, and walked into the foyer. The last thing I remember is hearing the door slam behind me.

25
"Let us sing a song as we go along,
Let us banish care and strife,
That the world may know as we onward go,
There's a sunny side of life."
"On the Sunny Side of Life" - Tillet S.
Teddlie

My mind raced uncontrollably as it tried to
unsuccessfully make order of my situation. Lost
in contemplation, I considered the nature of evil,
and my thoughts turned quickly to cancer.
Uncontrolled, disorganized growth is the
definition of cancer that I find most easily
understood by my patients. Cancer remains the
scourge of human existence and, as medical
science continues to make advances in the
treatment of infectious disease, heart disease,

and trauma, cancer takes the center stage of scary things that can kill us. Our life expectations lengthen, and a life well-lived is no truer sign of the wealth of our people. But cancer brings the rich and the poor down equally and, like death, itself, is truly the great equalizer. If any disease could be considered evil, it would be cancer, and therefore it is commonly referred to as a malignancy.

Imagine all the different types of cancers. A cancer is named after the cell type from which it originates. So we have breast cancer, stomach cancer, prostate cancer, colon cancer, lung cancer, pancreatic cancer, thyroid cancer, and more. Our understanding is that it only takes one cell to transform into cancer and, if our immune system is unable to destroy that cell, it will begin to replicate at an uncontrollable rate. These new cancer cells don't form viable tissues, but instead release a factor into the body that drives blood flow to the tumor, which feeds it the nutrients it needs to keep growing uncontrollably.

If we were to collect all the different cancers that are diagnosed each year in America into a giant pie graph, most people would find it shocking that more than half of the millions of cancer patients suffer from skin cancer. It seems that most people know that it's out there, but few grasp the enormity of the skin cancer epidemic.

It wasn't always that way. In fact, skin cancer was a relatively rare occurrence 100 years ago and was mostly seen in sailors and farmers, those that labored in the sun. The idea of being tanned was looked down upon as undesirable by the people of that time. The style of the time was to wear protective clothing in the sun so that your skin would remain milky white. This was considered sexy and desirable. We often look back at the styles of that era as prudish, especially when we see pictures of the long-sleeved bathing suits of that time. Far from being some type of overwhelming modesty, instead it said more about the styles of the times.

Women wore bonnets, and men wore hats. A high class woman might carry a parasol in the daylight to protect her skin from the sun. Pale skin was seen as a marker for the leisure class, because certainly if you had to labor for your living you would be burnt and tanned by the sun. If, instead, you made your living by thinking or, even better, were so well off that you didn't have to work, then your skin would be untouched by the sun's damaging rays. This life of leisure was desirable to the people of that time, and style followed what was desirable, and desirability is what makes things sexy.

Things changed in the 1920's when French designer Coco Chanel made an appearance at the French Riviera with a full-bodied sun tan. She reportedly stated that she had nothing better to do but lie around on the Duke of Westminster's yacht. This avowal of leisure time from a society fashion plate influenced the masses into believing that having a full bodied sun tan was desirable and therefore sexy.

This change in the public's perspective of what was sexy changed the way life was enjoyed for the next century. Over that time period, our bathing suits became smaller and smaller, and the skin cancer rate became higher and higher.

Patients often don't believe me that this skin cancer epidemic is based on style and behavior. They have their own theories of ozone depletion and global warming. I usually seal their grasp of the issue by pointing out that we culturally think of a tan as sexy except in one particular instance. And I ask them, "What type of tan is not sexy and therefore not desirable?" It doesn't take them long to answer that it is a "farmer's tan." And they quickly realize that this is a subject of scorn, because it's a working class tan and not a sign of a life of leisure. Since a life of leisure is what everyone desires, that's what makes it sexy.

So sex and desirability were driving the skin cancer epidemic and were what kept dermatologists like me working hard at my specialty. Certainly sex and desirability were also driving the cosmetic surgery industry, as well; in fact, it was their stock-in-trade.

By this reasoning, being a dermatologist is probably the sexiest specialty in the medical field. I know my colleagues in plastic surgery, urology, and gynecology would have a few bones of contention about this, but I think you can see my point.

The point of my diatribe is not to elevate the dermatologist to some kind of pedestal, but to emphasize the real burden of skin cancer on society and the special experts who treat it.

Dermatologists are the experts on the structure and function of the skin, hair, nails, and mucous membranes, and of their diseases. It is often said that the skin is the largest organ of the human body, and it's the protective wrapping of the body from the outside environment. Dermatologists have become the experts on protecting their patients from skin cancer.

Patients and colleagues alike are often confused by our specialty, and I've been asked on many occasions if I was in fact a "real doctor". I have been told by my hospital-based brethren in other specialties that dermatologists "are not." Whether this is good-natured ribbing or real jealousy is uncertain, but we certainly are real physicians.

To become a dermatologist, we must graduate from medical school, complete a one year internship, then finish a three-year dermatology residency. During this training we see multitudes of patients with usual and unusual skin diseases, and we are taught to recognize their clues to diagnose them. Having the ability to diagnose the problem is what allows us to prescribe the treatment that will help our patient most.

Sir Arthur Conan Doyle, a physician himself, was believed to pattern his greatest character, the master sleuth Sherlock Holmes, after his friend and teacher, Dr. Joseph Bell, a renowned diagnostician and dermatologist. Holmes used his deductive skills to fight the forces of evil.

I had tried to use my diagnostic skills and understanding of human nature to help Frank fight the evil forces that had killed the once beautiful Lourdes Rivera. Call it hubris, passion, or just plain curiosity, but, by getting involved in this case, I had reawakened a malignancy from my past, and that evil had apparently spread.

26
"There's a dark and a troubled side of life
There's a bright and a sunny side, too"
"Keep on the Sunny Side of Life" - Ada
Blenkhorn

I awoke with a pounding headache like I've never experienced before. My mouth felt dry, and a mountain of bitter grit coated my tongue. I opened my eyes to find myself seated in one of our kitchen chairs, and my hands were restrained behind my back. I spit whatever was in my mouth out with a force strong enough to send my spittle across the kitchen to the microwave oven.

A dark voice from my past laughed with pride and spoke to me in Spanish.

"My old friend finally awakens."

I turned my aching head to follow the voice and met eyes with the dreaded Emeliano, who sat comfortably on the granite countertop of our kitchen's island table. He smoked a cigar and appeared quite satisfied with himself.

I remembered that the police were stationed outside the house so I screamed, "Help! Help me!"

Emeliano laughed.

"There's no use in screaming, el doctor. The police officers can't hear you. A big rich house like yours keeps its secrets to itself."

He was right, our house was virtually soundproofed to prevent outside noise from bothering us. My thoughts immediately turned to Christina and the children, and I said a silent prayer that they had followed my instructions and remained locked inside the safe room. Emeliano noticed my attention drifting away, and he came at me.

"I would think that I would have your full attention, el doctor."

He took his cigar out of his mouth and brought the lit end toward my right eye. I turned my head away from him.

"What do you want?" I asked in Spanish.

He planted the burning ember of the cigar into my right temple and let it cook. I struggled to move my head, but he used his other hand to hold me steady. I believe I tried to hold back a scream, but I know that I didn't.

"I want your complete attention, el doctor."

"You got it." I resigned myself.

Emeliano smiled the grin of a hungry great white shark - all teeth, but no humor in the eyes. There was just an unspeakable absence of any sort of human decency. He was what medical professionals call a sociopath, and the absence of genuine emotion had set him on a one-way path of evil.

Doctors learn quickly how to operate in stressful situations because, when someone else's life hangs in the balance, it's important that you can act logically and quickly and put your emotions on hold. Controlling this flight or fight reaction is all well and good when you're not the patient, and I think most doctors would agree that doctors make the worst patients. That being said, I was still surprised when I felt my bladder relax, and I pissed myself.

I looked down in horror to see the warm feeling wetting my pants wasn't urine, but blood. I looked back up to Emeliano.

"I poisoned you like the rat you are, el doctor." He laughed. "I've been planning to take my revenge upon you ever since I arrived in Miami. I've studied the layout of your home, and I know how to get in and out of here without being noticed. I want to reassure you that I also have made plans for my revenge upon your lovely wife."

At the mention of Christina, my mind raced with hope for her safety. I began to feel my analytical skills come to the forefront, my heartbeat slowed, and I stoked my resolve.

"If I'm just going to die of poison, why are you still here? Some perverse kind of enjoyment?"

Nothing seemed to wipe that twisted toothy smile off his face. My eyes were instinctively drawn to an unusual mole on his left ear.

"I'm certainly enjoying this, el doctor. But you're right. I was ready to go, but I began to wonder about something. I couldn't get it out of my head that something wasn't right."

"None of this is right, Emeliano."

He bristled a little when I used his name.

"Why did you come to the plastic surgery reception? I recognized your name on our guest list and I wondered what you were doing there."

"It was a doctor party. I'm a doctor," I answered as if speaking to a child.

"Then how come you didn't drink any of the cocktails at the reception? Who told you we had drugged the liquor?"

He was coming toward me with his cigar again.

"Are you kidding me?" I put on a brave face since I knew I was going to die anyway.

"You'll tell me, el doctor." He pulled the cigar from his mouth, stared at the glowing tip, then looked into my face. His threat was clear.

I noticed some movement behind Emeliano and saw my dog silently watching us from under Christina's desk.

"Emeliano, I'll tell you, of course. But before I do, you must let me look at that mole on your ear."

Emeliano laughed and spoke to me sarcastically.

"Are you going to help me out now, el doctor? Am I your friend now?"

"It's just my training, Emeliano, but believe me I would love to see you die from melanoma."

He stopped smiling.

"You think this is a melanoma?" He leaned toward me.

I shifted the chair, feigning to get a better look at his ear, but really so I could let the dog see my hands.

"I think you should get it removed."

"Doctor Roto wanted to take it off too, but I thought it would hurt."

I looked up at his dead shark eyes and made a fist with my right hand.

"You'll only feel a little pinch!"

Upon hearing her name, my silent dog looked at my fist signal, leaped from under the desk, and brought the full weight of her 110 pounds down upon Emeliano's neck. As he was leaning in to show me his ear, he was off-balance to begin with.

I remember taking Little Pinch on a camping trip in North Florida where she captured and pinned a wild boar. Taking down Emeliano was much easier. She clamped her mostly pitbull-like jaws around his neck and held him firmly on the floor. A small trickle of blood dripped from where her lips touched his neck. Emeliano whimpered like a little girl.

"Help me, el doctor," he implored.

Little Pinch raised her eyes to me and gave me a quizzical look like she was asking *Well, are you going to let me eat him*?

I was still tied to the chair and in no state to get myself free. I had resigned myself to my death before Little Pinch had taken my oppressor down. My pants were soaked with my own blood and urine, and I could feel my nose running. The poison was already working its wonders. Despite the unlikelihood of my survival, I had some questions that I needed answered.

"Lourdes Rivera?" I asked.

Emeliano stopped whimpering, and his strange poignant silence accentuated the surreal situation of a silent dog holding this man pinned to my kitchen floor while I sat tied to a chair covered in more and more of my own blood.

"What about her?" he squeaked.

"Why did you kill her?" I asked.

"She deserved to die." He continued, "The bitch came to Doctor Roto's clinic, and she wasn't interested in becoming a hostess, so she paid full price for the work she had done."

He stopped.

"So?" I prodded.

"El doctor, you're stuck in that chair, and you're going to die if you don't get to a hospital. Maybe you should call off your dog, and I'll be able to untie you."

It was my turn to laugh. "Lourdes Rivera. Why did she deserve to die?"

"I told you, el doctor. She refused an offer to become part of the stable."

"So every woman who comes to Doctor Roto's clinic is supposed to join the stable?"

"No, no, of course not. We offer the truly beautiful clients the opportunity of free cosmetic surgery and a well-paying job as a hostess."

"So Lourdes didn't want to do it. So what?"

"Well, after her recovery, we had a party for the patients and many of the hostesses. Many big shots like to come to the party for the fun. Let's just say she offended some of the leadership with her views on Cuba and President Castro at the party, and she rebuffed the advances of an important man."

"Like Uncle Hugo?"

"Do not make light of our great president, el doctor."

I imagined a bizarre sordid sexcapade where communist leaders are entertained by the stable of hostesses from Doctor Roto's clinic.

"So she turned down the advances of a fat old man. Is that now a reason to kill her?"

"She made a stink at the party and when she returned to Miami, she got a tattoo. A tattoo of the old horse of Venezuela, not the new horse, then she got some modeling deals and a picture of her with that tattoo showed up in some magazines in our country and drew the attention of leadership."

I understood now. This free-thinking American girl whose parents escaped the nightmare of Castro's Cuba visits Venezuela hoping to get cheap cosmetic surgery. She has a bad experience and stages her own private rebellion by getting a tattoo of the pre-Chavez horse emblazoned just above her rump.

My head began to hurt worse because my blood pressure most surely was rising. I asked my final question.

"Why did you cut off her tattoo?"

Emeliano squeaked a malevolent giggle. "Leadership wanted a souvenir."

I looked into Little Pinch's eyes, and she looked to my hand. I brought my index finger and middle finger together like a scissors snap. I heard the bones make a sickening crunch in her powerful jaws, and I looked away.

I leaned the chair I was sitting in to its side and tipped it over with enough force that the back leg broke off in the fall. I hit the floor with a slap, and my feet were still tied to the front legs of the chair. My hands were behind me. I slammed the back of the wooden chair into the kitchen cabinets, and the right side splintered. I looked over at Little Pinch, who was watching me comfortably while grooming her paws. Emeliano lay on his back in an ever-widening pool of blood.

I was able to lift my arms away from the back of the broken chair. Though my wrists were tied, I was able to fish my cell phone from my pocket. Laying it upon the floor, I used the touch screen to call 9-11.

I gave the operator the address and told her that I was poisoned and that I needed Vitamin K. I lay on the floor and wept tears of blood for Lourdes Rivera, my dog, and my predicament. I didn't waste a tear on Emeliano.

27
"You'll never know dear,
How much I love you,
Please don't take my sunshine away!"
"You Are My Sunshine" - Jimmie Davis &
Charles Mitchell

I awoke in a private room at Mt. Sinai Hospital. At my bedside was Doctor Mario Barquin, who smiled at me as my eyes opened.

"I'm so happy you've rejoined us. Leave it to you to get me to come to work when I'm having the worst hangover of my life. But we're not alone ..."

He motioned with his arm, and I saw Christina and the kids seated beside the bed. My heart soared.

"Hey, Sweetie." I smiled.

"Good afternoon, sleepyhead." She grasped my hand and kissed me. I looked down at the purple bruising that covered my hands.

"My God," I whispered.

"You should see your face," Christina said with a nervous laugh and handed me a mirror.

I looked at an unrecognizable visage of myself. My eyelids were swollen, and my face was purple. There was crusted blood on my nostrils and the corners of my mouth. On my right temple was a bandage where Emeliano's cigar had burned me.

"They found you on the floor of the kitchen, and the doctors think the trauma caused by your chair breaking caused most of the bruising." She began to cry.

"Don't worry, Sweetie. It's going to be all right."

My doctor's mind took over.

"I'll probably look close to normal in about a week."

I gripped her hand and looked over at the children. Danielle's eyes threw open wide when she looked at me, then she looked away quickly. Lizard jumped right up on the bed with me, then asked if it hurt.

"It's better because you guys are here. Don't worry, Danielle." I reached out for her hand, and she took it.

"Thank God the dog was there, but I thought you had her with you in the safe room."

"I did, but when I heard the door slam, I figured you were home, so I let Little Pinch out to meet you."

"You're my guardian angel."

Lizard looked at me with awe and wonder. "Dad, Uncle Frank and the police are here to talk with you."

I looked over at the door and saw Frank peek in.

"Mind if I come in?" he whispered.

Christina shot him a dirty look.

"Look what you did to my husband. Where was your police protection?"

Frank threw up his hands.

"I know, I know, Christina. If anyone could be as mad about this as you, it would be me."

He reached out to put his hand on mine and Christina's. He looked at the state of me, and tears began to well in his eyes.

"If there's anything I can do to make up for this, please just ask."

I thought about how this whole sordid affair began with Frank asking about tattoos and how I didn't think the disfigurement of Lourdes Rivera had been about a murderer collecting trophies. I had been wrong, and Frank had been right. But this whole investigation had exposed a senseless plot fueled by the hypocrisy of communists selling cosmetic surgery as a capitalist enterprise and the base rewards of using women as objects for illicit sex. I sat there struck by the evil men do, and I wondered if I had made any difference at all.

I looked at Christina and the kids and thought of their future in a world so twisted and rotten. I turned back to Frank.

"I want you to get me a badge. Or do I have to call Broder?"

Prepare for the next exciting novel about Doctor Harry Poe, the Skinvestigator- "Rash Guard"

An excerpt from the forthcoming

Book Two of the
Sunshine State Trilogy

the
SKINVESTIGATOR

RASH
GUARD

TERRY CRONIN

The
Skinvestigator

Rash Guard

TERRY CRONIN

1
"Sunshine of Your Love" - Cream

The surf sucks on Miami Beach, Gabriella thought as she paddled her board back out into the line-up. She used to love surfing, the sun, the water, and the athleticism. When she was growing up in Brazil, it was the most exciting part of her life. It also gave her a sense of peace and was the closest she ever got to a religious experience. Now everything sucked.

She wasn't enjoying herself, and she wondered why she ever wasted so much of her time surfing. The little voice in her head told her there was only one thing that would make her feel better. She told herself that she listened to that little voice too much, but she knew her efforts were futile.

She wasn't at the beach to have fun; she was working. She needed money to support her drug habit, and her drug of choice was crystal meth.

Her boyfriend Luis told her that tourists love surfer girls and that she should be able to get some action at the beach hotel resorts. She used to think a lot about Luis and how great he was, but now she thought Luis sucked, too. When she put her bathing suit on, Luis told her, "No one is gonna look twice at a skanky tweeker like you." Gabriella hadn't looked in the mirror in a while, so she was surprised at what looked back at her. She was much skinnier than she remembered, and her chest and back were covered in some kind of rash.

Luis threw a shirt at her, and she slipped it on over her head. It was a surf shirt made of Lycra and fit her snugly. She looked in the mirror and smiled at her womanly figure. She didn't bother to brush her teeth.

She had worn a shirt like this many times when she used to compete in surf contests. They're called "rash guards" to prevent the wax on the surfboard from irritating your chest. She laughed to herself that her rash guard was now protecting others from seeing her nasty rash.

The little voice inside her head told her that she'd feel better if she made some money. She spotted a fat older man on the beach and tried to look sexy as she made her way out of the water in his direction.

2
"Sunshine" - Jack Johnson

I was tired.

It was another wonderful day of seeing patients one after another. I'm a dermatologist which, if you don't know, is a doctor of the skin. Dermatologists are the experts on skin disease and, although I was trained to treat thousands of skin problems, working in sunny South Florida had made my practice almost entirely devoted to treating one subset of disease - skin cancer. Skin cancer has reached an epidemic in Florida, and I was seeing patient after patient with the same symptoms - changing moles, non-healing sores, and horny crusts on their skin. It's a great thing to be busy, but after a whole day of talking to people I get burnt out. I looked forward to having dinner with my wife and kids and decompressing at home.

That wasn't going to happen.

My cell phone rang with the suspenseful ring tone which played the theme music from the old police show "Dragnet," and I knew Frank was calling.

"What's up, Doc?" he asked. Frank thinks he's a comedian. He's not. He's a detective with the Miami Metro Police and a damn good one. We've been friends since high school, and I've watched his career rise with a bit of personal pride. I always knew Frank was a truly great man, and I was happy to see the world finally recognizing his talents.

Frank was currently sitting at the bottom of my wife Christina's estimation, because she felt he had almost gotten me killed. Christina held a lot against Frank. He had said and done some things before we got married that hurt our relationship, and she's never truly forgiven him for it.

My near-death experience was the final straw, and Christina had little use for Frank. Whenever his name came up, her standing comment was, "Stay away from him."

I couldn't do that. He was truly one of my best friends, and I knew I could always count on him. I wanted to be just as good a friend to Frank as he was to me. As I was growing up, my mother always told me that a true friend was a rare person to find, and what makes them true is that they can be counted on during the good times and the bad.

We had just come through a really bad time. Frank had asked me to help with a murder case dealing with tattoos, because he thought my dermatologic expertise could add to the investigation. We had uncovered a bizarre cosmetic surgery enterprise run by the Venezuelan government, and I nearly got killed by the murderer we were searching for.

Despite the protection of the Miami Metro Police, the murderer had made it into my home, tortured, and poisoned me. Thanks to my beloved wife and my dog, Little Pinch, I was saved from an early grave.

The newspapers had made a big deal about my home invasion, and the American Kennel Club recognized my dog as a hero. The story in the paper called "Little Pinch" a "giant bundle of muscles and teeth with a heart of gold." I would have to agree. I worried that her experience with the killer might change her sweet disposition. It had certainly changed mine.

I had been struck by the evil men do and the world I was raising my children in, and I had decided that I wanted to help the detective branch of the Miami Metro PD with my deductive skills. I had demanded a badge.

Frank thought this was ridiculous, as it takes a long time for an officer to rise through the ranks to become a detective. His boss, Commander Jimenez, found the idea laughable and wouldn't even consider it. That was when I played my trump card -- Broder.

Broder was my neighbor and, other than Christina and Frank, my best friend. He was also the most low down ambulance-chasing attorney that people had ever seen. Believe me, those who lived in South Florida had seen his advertisements on the back of every phone book, every billboard, and on heavy rotation on late night cable TV. "Slip and fall? Then you must call your attorney — Gabriel Broder!"

Both Frank and Jimenez knew his reputation as a shark, and they also knew of my relationship with him. So by just the mention of his name, they capitulated and gave me a detective shield.

Frank understood my motivations and was happy to have my help, but my relationship with Jimenez had gotten decidedly frosty. He gave me my shield, but he made sure that it was only valid for one year and that I only got paid as a first-year rookie for time served.

I wasn't doing it for the money. I knew that my training and time were valuable to the police, and now I would have to prove it. Jimenez had taken me into his office to have me sign paperwork absolving the department of any wrongdoing in the previous case, and he had assured me that this admission would not affect my current position in the department.   He became incredibly annoyed when I told him that I appreciated his assurances but would also need that in writing. To his credit he gave me a written and notarized assurance that I would be a detective with the force for the next year and, until that time, I would not be subject to removal of my rank or badge, barring wrong-doing.

He asked me if everything appeared in order, and when I agreed, he sat down, and looked me in the eye.

"Look, Doc, I get why you think you should do this and I understand that you think you can help."

"There's a big "But" coming soon I imagine." I smiled.

"But you've got to realize that police work is just that -- "work". The only thing I can think is that you've been reading too many detective novels to think this is something you want to do."

"I want to help wherever I can," I offered.

"That's fair," he said, "When a perpetrator needs a Botox injection, I know who I'll call."

"Listen, Commander, I get it. You don't think I belong here. That I haven't earned it. But try to warm to the idea that I am only offering my help. If I can't help or I'm not useful, we'll find out quickly."

"Look Doc, I'm gonna tell you this once and then we'll forget this conversation ever happened. I get that you're a smart doctor and that you went to school for a long time but that doesn't make you an expert on anything other than practicing medicine. You're acting like you're God's gift to police work and you're basically like a child who thinks they have ideas that can help out the space program."

"It's not like that. I'm like a consultant."

"Oh no, you're wrong. A consultant doesn't get a badge so it is like that. Listen, you've got friends in high places so we'll work with you but let's keep this whole deal low profile. I deal with bureaucrats, politicians, and journalists all day long and I can tell you if this gets out we will have no end of trouble. Everyone wants to be a detective these days and the process isn't easy for a reason. It's tough."

So here I was with my badge and my desire to help and Frank was calling me.

"I'm doing great, my man, not much going on here. How are you?" I asked him over my cell phone.

"I've been told I'm stunning," Frank laughed. "Look Doc, I'm calling because Coltrane has a body and he's got some questions for our newest detective."

This sounded great to me until Frank laughed again.

"What are you laughing at?" I bristled.

"I was just thinking about Jimenez' face when you turn in your hours."

In fact, it only took me minutes to figure it out, but I'm getting ahead of myself.

3
"(Always Be My) Sunshine" - Jay-Z

The coroner's office of Dade County is an amazing edifice. The government tried its best to dress it up but it still gave me a creepy feeling despite its warm colors and modern architecture.

It reminded me of when a criminal attorney makes his client dress up for court in a suit. The suspect may have his haircut, his teeth brushed, and may be able to pull off a coat and tie so that he appears like a respectable businessman but, underneath the façade, he is still a crook. Innocent until proven guilty, of course. Now that I was in law enforcement these important little things needed to be stated and remembered.

Frank and I had come to the coroner's office to see Coltrane. I have described him in the past as a ghoul but that isn't quite fair. In fact, when he smiled, he reminded me of a big teddy bear. However when he was annoyed, he took on the likeness of a hairy goblin straight out of "The Lord of the Rings".

He looked particularly annoyed when we walked into the ridiculously cold morgue.

"It's about time, detectives!" He scowled.

I felt a little pride well up inside of me just for being referred to a s a detective. Frank only laughed.

"I hope you're not wasting our time, Coltrane," Frank retorted. "What up, buttercup?"

"Believe it or not, I needed a dermatology consult so I was hoping Miami's newest Detective Poe could help me ... and you could just baby-sit us."

"If I'm baby-sitting you Coltrane, we may need to put a call into child protective services even before I start."

"If I could interrupt you two lovebirds," I said butting in to save the day, "why don't you tell us about the victim, Coltrane?"

Coltrane smiled and everything was teddy bears from then on.

"Sure, Doc. The victim's name is Gabriella Amado, 22 years old, and she came to the US on a student visa from Brazil three years ago. Near as I can tell she finished a semester at Florida Atlantic University and then fell off their radar. She was found dumped in a canal in Kendall and it appears she died from an overdose of both OxyContin and methamphetamine. Not too many clues to go on but she was wearing a water-resistant shirt and there was a waxy material imbedded in the fabric on her chest which appears to be surf wax."

"What did you want me for?" I asked.

"Let me show you."

Coltrane walked us over to a rolling metal table and undraped the corpse. On the table lay the mortal remains of Gabriella. She must have been pretty at one time but now it appeared she had been run ragged.

The first thing I noticed was cachexia or unhealthy thinness. This was usually seen in patients wasting away from malnutrition, the ravages of cancer, or an eating disorder. Her hips and ribs were too prominent and her muscles were wasted. She had very little if any body fat.

On her face were self-inflicted sores which the French would call "*acne de jeunnes filles*" which is a description of acne in young girls. This process is found often secondarily infected because the young girl squeezes and picks her face compulsively. This victim's face was worse than that with signs of scarring and impetigo from her chronic picking. This clue coupled with her neglected dentition was a classic look for a crystal meth addict.

She had several tattoos on her arms. A band of barb wire encircled her left arm and a peace sign showed just above her mons pubis. Scattered over her chest were coin-shaped patches of redness and as I looked at them closely I asked Coltrane for gloves.

I pulled the gloves over my hands and reached out to take the hand of the poor dead girl before me. I turned her hand over despite her rigidity and found the same nickel and dime sized lesions on her palm.

Frank and Coltrane looked at me expectantly and I smiled.

"I think I can help you Coltrane."

"Yes?" He waited as I relished their expectancy.

"It's syphilis."

Also by Terry Cronin

Spread the word about
**The Skinvestigator and
The Sunshine State Trilogy!**

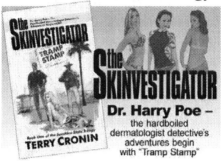

Book 1: Tramp Stamp
Book 2: Rash Guard
Book 3: Sun Burn